Lucky Shoes

Lucky Shoes

Ray Millholland

WILDSIDE PRESS

Lucky Shoes

Chapter 1

Andy Carter walked slowly out of the principal's office at Riverford High School with his class assignment card for the fall semester in his hand. In spite of the fact that it was a beautiful September day and the corridor was filled with familiar faces of classmates smiling and calling out to him as they scurried past, Andy had that "Oh, me!" feeling inside.

And all because of the change that Mr. McCall, the principal, had just made on his assignment card! This was one of those mix-ups that left a fellow helpless to do anything about it. In fact, Mr. McCall, who had charge of smoothing out conflicts in assignments, had shown Andy that even *he* was not able to repair the damage.

The whole thing had started back in June, at the end of Andy's junior year, when he definitely decided that he was going on to college and study engineering. He had talked the matter over with Mr. Stark, the shop and mechanical drawing teacher, and Mr. Stark had told him that, by all means, he should take machine shop in his senior year.

Andy took another look at the changes on his assignment card and groaned—out loud this time, "Oh, my aching arches!"

Right on top of that Andy got a hard poke in the ribs from another member of the senior class, Ted Hall. Ted always wore two things—a pair of spectacles with thick lenses and a brisk but friendly smile for everybody.

Ted said, "If you need a doctor, I'm your man. I've

been taping football ankles and rubbing linament on Charley horses so long that I think I could take out your appendix if you were game enough to trust me. Stick out your tongue and say '*Ah!*'"

But not even the teasing of the football team's student manager could make Andy smile just then. He handed Ted his assignment card and said, "Operate on this if you're that good a doctor. They've just switched my machine shop class from the first and second periods to the seventh and eighth. That means I don't get out of class until three-thirty, and football practice starts at two-thirty."

Andy did not have to tell Ted what that meant. Both of them had received a copy of the same letter which the new coach, Mr. Dorman, had sent to members of last year's football squad, including the freshmen, who would now be sophomores and eligible to win places on the varsity.

"To all boys intending to turn out for football this fall," Coach Dorman's letter began. "This is a get-acquainted letter. I have been appointed your new coach, so naturally you are wondering what sort of a person I am.

"Since I come from another state and there is no one at Riverford High who knows me, I will tell you what sort of a person I *try* to be. No one, of course, knows exactly what sort of person he really is, but I hope that by the end of the football season you will have decided that, considering everything, I'm not such a bad guy, after all.

"Now let's start from there. In the first place, every boy who takes care to arrange his schedule so that he can report regularly every day for practice, *immediately after two-thirty,* and gives his level best, is going to get all the help toward winning his varsity letter that I can give him.

"Next, I have no favorites. Everybody starts with a clean slate for this season. Any boy who was a star last year and thinks he can win a place on the varsity this year without giving his best, *every minute of practice every day,* is sure to find that some other fellow—a plugger—is in the starting line-up while he warms the substitute bench.

"Although I teach the same system used by your former loved coach, Mr. Skiles, I do not promise we will win the conference championship this year or even next. This may be a disappointment to you juniors and seniors, but I hope you will put just that much more 'try' into your practice and actual game playing.

"This letter is long enough for the time being. We will get better acquainted as the season progresses. Remember—if we take the measure of that hard-cracking Mansfield High team in the last game of the season, it won't be such a bad year, after all!

"With best personal wishes,

"JOHN DORMAN,

"Coach."

At the time Andy Carter received his copy of the new coach's letter he felt sure that Mr. Dorman was a real straight-talking square shooter. And right up to the time Mr. McCall, the principal, had told him about the changes in his study hours, Andy had been confident that he was at last going to win his varsity football letter, for sure, in his senior year.

But all that was changed now. Right there, in black and white, in the new coach's letter was fair warning, *that only those boys who reported for practice every day at the beginning of the seventh class hour would have the ghost of a chance to make the first-string varsity!*

Ted Hall seemed to have the same idea, too. He took one look at Andy's assignment schedule—saw that Andy would be in a machine shop class during the seventh and eighth periods—and said, "This is what needs an emergency operation, not you. See Mr. Stark right away and get him to switch you to his morning machine shop class."

Andy shook his head. "I'm signed up for College Algebra. Only twelve seniors are taking that course, so I can't juggle my schedule and get into a morning machine shop class." Slowly he took back his schedule from his friend Ted Hall. "I'm sunk—no varsity letter for me."

"Don't start looking for a crying towel yet," said Ted briskly. He gave Andy a steady look through the thick lenses of his eyeglasses. "You'll have enough credits to graduate next June *even if you drop machine shop entirely.*"

Again Andy shook his head, but not quite so positively this time. "Everybody, including my father, Mr. McCall, and Mr. Stark, says I should take machine shop if I plan to study engineering in college."

The bell for the next class hour began ringing. Ted Hall gave Andy an encouraging thump on the chest with the back of his hand and said, "Keep your chin off your belt buckle, old horse. You've got until Wednesday to decide about dropping machine shop. Don't do anything foolish before then." As Ted hurried off he flung a wink back over his shoulder. "See you for football practice tonight. I got a swell new pair of shoes saved out for you!"

Class periods on the opening day of the fall semester at Riverford High were shorter than usual. There was just time enough for the teacher to take down the names of the pupils and announce the textbook which will be used. Then the bell would ring and the corridors would be filled again with pupils hurrying to their next class.

Coach Dorman had taken advantage of these short class periods on opening day to issue a call to all football candidates to report to the gymnasium locker room at one-thirty, when practice uniforms would be issued.

By the time Andy got out of his short machine shop class, most of the other seniors were already in the locker room. They knew from experience how important it was to get there early so that they could get a good pair of shoes—the most important thing—that fitted their feet, as well as first pick of pants, jerseys, and shoulder pads.

Immediately Andy went to the shoe bin and started hunting for a pair of shoes that would fit him. The shoes had become all mixed up by then. All he could find was one right-foot shoe his size that was in serviceable condition.

Then Ted Hall nudged him in the ribs and said in a confidential undertone, "Never mind digging through that junk, Andy. I've got booties for your little number tens saved out for you."

Ted climbed up on a stool and with his short arms

began groping for the promised shoes, far back out of sight on top a row of steel lockers. Meanwhile Andy had peeled off his shirt and was trying on a set of shoulder pads for size. Right next to where Andy was seated on one of the long dressing benches, two sophomores were good-naturedly scuffling with each other.

Out of the corner of his eye Andy saw one of the sophomores give the other a quick push that sent the boy reeling back into the stool on which Ted was standing on his tiptoes.

The stool went flying out from under Ted. With a quick dive Andy flung his body across a hard bench over the spot where the back of Ted's head was about to strike. Ted landed on him with an indignant grunt and bounced to his feet.

Just then Andy felt a firm hand on his arm, and Coach Dorman said, "What's your name, Son?"

"Andy Carter, sir," said Andy.

Coach Dorman nodded approvingly. "I like the way you think fast, Carter. If you hadn't broken that boy's fall with your body, he might have received a serious head injury." Then the coach turned sternly to the others. "There will be no more horseplay in the locker room from now on. The next offender will be asked to turn in his uniform, and I don't care whether he is a star or a scrub. The playing field is the only place for rough-and-tumble."

Coach Dorman swept the squad with another stern look, then left the locker room.

Ted Hall straightened up his glasses, which had been dangling from his right ear, and grinned at Andy. "You owe me one of Wally's Banana Split Specials for this.

My backward-dive act got you a swell introduction to the new coach."

Ken Blair, a junior, came over and said to Andy, "I was nearer to that bench than you were, Andy. But you beat me to it. All I ask is that you'll be in the backfield blocking for me this year. And I promise to block my best for you when you're carrying the ball."

Ken, though an inch taller than Andy, was a year younger. Toward the end of the previous football season he had developed rapidly as a triple-threat backfield man.

But somehow Andy had never really cottoned to Ken. For one thing, it had been pretty hard to sit on the substitute bench as a junior last year and watch a sophomore winning the varsity letter that Andy was trying for.

Down in his heart, of course, Andy knew that Ken—last year, at least—had been the better backfield man. But this year Andy had been working hard all summer, swinging a pick and shovel with a construction gang and practicing forward passing—all with the determination to report for his last season of football in the best physical condition of any man on the squad. And that included Ken, one of those unusual boys who always seem to be in perfect physical condition.

So, for the moment, Andy was thrown for a one-yard mental loss by Ken's neat little speech. All he could think of to say was, "Thanks, and the same to you."

Ken did not seem to mind either the shortness of Andy's reply or the gruff tone in which it was spoken as he turned and walked out of the locker room, headed for the practice field with a football in his skillful hands.

Ted Hall, who always managed to see what was

going on, waited until all the rest of the squad had left the locker room; then, just as Andy's eyes showed through the jersey that he was pulling on, said, "Old horse, *I* know you didn't mean it that way, but to the rest of the gang it sounded as if you were still sore at Ken for beating your time last year."

"What am I supposed to do now?" retorted Andy, feeling more uncomfortable than ever. "Should I run up to Ken in front of the whole squad and kiss him to show how much I really think of the guy as a football player?"

"For crying out loud," said Ted in that disgusted tone that only a close friend dare use (Incidentally, Ted could use that tone on any member of the squad, including Ken Blair, without being resented.), "this isn't *last* year. We've got a new coach; we've got more letter men and game-experienced backs, like you, back this year than we've ever had. *This* year we've got the best chance of winning the conference championship by beating Mansfield that we ever had."

Ted gave Andy an emphasizing poke in the ribs with a stubby forefinger, adding, "But it is going to take better team spirit than we had last year to do it. And that's your main job, old horse. You've got to show these sophomores and juniors a real sample of team spirit—all the time, every minute, I mean."

Ted started to add another point, but Andy cut him off with a quick grin. "Get off your soapbox and come out and watch me show 'em."

Andy darted out of the locker room. He sprinted past the other leisurely jogging members of the squad and was the first to arrive at the practice field, where he finished with a dive and roll-over on the hard sun-baked turf that carried him to his feet again.

Coach Dorman, who had been standing back of a large tree at the east side line, shook his head at Andy and said, "I don't recommend that sort of thing this early in the season. Wait until you're in better condition."

Andy could have told the new coach that he had been practicing that dive and roll-over all summer long, and that he was in top playing physical condition already. But there was something in the look in the coach's eyes that made Andy feel he was being suspected of showing off to attract attention.

Andy said, "Yes, sir," and walked to the back to the circle of players who were now waiting expectantly for their first instructions from their new coach.

While Andy's ears were still red, a long arm draped itself over his shoulder and "Cornstalk" Shaw, a senior end, said with a mock groan, *"Don't* do that to me, my friend. I ache all over from just watching you hit the dirt like that. I've got at least two caved-in ribs, I know. Doctor, doctor—I need a doctor, somebody! Even a dog and cat doctor will do!"

Out of the corner of his eye Andy saw Coach Dorman standing with his gray flannel-clad legs well apart and his big bronzed fists resting on his hips. From the way the coach's jaw was set, Andy had a sinking feeling in his stomach that Cornstalk was in for a sharp reprimand. Then he saw a twitching muscle at the corner of that firm mouth.

Coach Dorman dropped his hands from his hips and said crisply to Cornstalk, "If you can still clown like that at the end of the tough season ahead of us, Son, I'll be pleasantly surprised."

The coach turned away abruptly, waved the squad onto the practice field, barking, "Line up, everybody, for grass drill!"

Led by their new coach, the squad went through fifteen minutes of bends, squats, and push-ups—and some new ones the boys had never seen before. The final exercise was to lie flat on their backs and bring their feet up over their heads, touching the ground with the tips of their shoes.

". . . nine—ten, halt!" barked the coach, then put his hands back of his head, jerked his heels under his body, and stood erect.

A few boys with a little breath left tried to do it too, but they all failed and had to roll over on their knees in order to stand up—including Andy.

Standing right back of Andy was Cornstalk. But this time the tall end was careful not to allow his remarks to be overheard by the coach. "This is probably my last day on earth. I have a feeling that our new coach is going to eat me for supper and then throw my picked bones to the cat. He just doesn't appreciate humor—my style, anyhow."

Andy tossed a reassuring grin over his shoulder. "Cheer up, Cornstalk, I'll save your life as soon as I can get my hands on a football."

Andy kept his rescue plans to himself until after Coach Dorman had emptied a bag of practice footballs on the ground, saying, "I want to see what you backs and ends can do with these things."

Andy pounced on one of the better-conditioned balls

and fitted it into his throwing hand. He nodded to Corn-stalk. "Get going!"

Downfield sped Cornstalk in that lumbering gallop of his. Andy waited with the ball cocked back of his ear until a split second before Cornstalk made his sharp break to the left. Then he let go with a long, high pass.

It was not a particularly accurate pass; and it looked —for a moment, at least—as though it were going to soar far over Cornstalk's head and out of his reach. But suddenly the lanky end put on a fresh burst of speed. Up—up he went into the air. The ball smacked into Cornstalk's hands and he came down, running, with it.

Out of the corner of his eye Andy watched to see how Coach Dorman liked that circus catch by Corn-stalk. But although the coach was facing in that direc-tion at the time he seemed to be concentrating on show-ing a lineman how to use his hands on defense. At any rate, he did not give Cornstalk as much as a side glance as the lanky end came lumbering back up the field.

Other candidates for end positions were lined up, one back of the other, and yelling "Pass! Pass!" at Andy.

He threw five more long ones, but they all sailed wide of vainly lunging receivers and went out of bounds.

Suddenly Coach Dorman turned away from the line-men he had been instructing and walked toward Andy, whose attention, right then, was concentrated on hitting Cornstalk—up for his second turn at pass catching.

This one was straight down the middle again. It was the longest pass Andy had made that day. But the moment the ball left his hand he was sure that it would be far out of Cornstalk's reach, because he had thrown it to his receiver's blind side!

Cornstalk kept looking over his right shoulder for the ball; then, like a stepladder caught in a cyclone, he whirled and leaped high into the air—higher than Andy had even seen him go before.

The fact that Cornstalk came down with the ball in his hands did not seem to give him any pleasure whatsoever. He threw the ball back at Andy and yelled, "What are you trying to do—twist my head off?"

Just then Coach Dorman tapped Andy on the shoulder, saying, "Son, your long passes remind me of a cannon in my battery during the war. That thing could pitch a shell farther than any other gun we had. But the sight was bent and we couldn't hit a flock of barns with it from here to the goal line. When we pulled out the next morning to chase the enemy we left that poor-shooting gun behind."

Coach Dorman walked away from Andy and over to where Ken Blair was throwing passes to another group of ends. Andy heard him say, "Blair, you're leading them nicely with those short passes, but throw them a little higher. Make your receiver leave his feet to catch the ball. A defensive back who gets between you and your receiver can't intercept high ones."

While Andy watched, Ken Blair threw several short but high passes. His receivers made awkward lunges with their hands for the ball—and missed.

After his fifth unsuccessful attempt Ken Blair turned to Coach Dorman and said, "What am I doing wrong now, Coach?"

"Keep throwing 'em just as you are," said Coach Dorman curtly. "Ends who expect to make the first team will have to learn to leave their feet for a pass, or they will warm the substitute bench and watch other boys play who will go up after 'em."

Shortly after that Coach Dorman blew his whistle and called the squad to him. "That's all for today," he told them. "Tomorrow afternoon we'll get down to hard work. I'll be giving out the first plays, so I want every one of you here promptly after the end of the sixth class period. Practice starts at two forty-five sharp. *No excuses for being late will be accepted.*"

Andy did not join the others in a free-for-all race to see who could get under the showers before all the hot water was gone. Instead he walked slowly, kicking at the cinders of the running track with his cleats. *You might just as well turn in your suit tonight,* he told himself, *because tomorrow afternoon, when you report late, after seventh- and eighth-period machine shop class——*

Suddenly Andy felt a friendly hand on his shoulder and heard Coach Dorman saying to him pleasantly, "I like to see a fellow put everything he's got into practice the way you did today. Cheer up! By the end of the week you'll be taking it in a breeze."

But before Andy could start on the subject of machine shop, Coach Dorman had turned off the path to the door leading into his small private office.

Chapter 2

As a rule, Mrs. Carter called her family to the dinner table at six o'clock, almost to the minute, every evening. But on the evening of the first day of the fall term of school she came into the living room and peered through the side window. Andy was looking over his new algebra textbook, and his sixteen-year-old sister, Susie, sat with one foot tucked under her while she listened to a radio program. That is, Susie was giving part of her attention to the radio program. But at least six times since six o'clock she had looked at the clock on the mantelpiece and had sighed hungrily.

There was a hint of worry in their mother's tone as she said, "I don't know what is keeping your father. If he doesn't come in five minutes, you children can have your supper."

Susie stole a quick look out the window and up the street, then said with her usual confidence, "Something has happened to Papa's old car. That's why he's late."

"I hope not," said Mrs. Carter with a little catch in her voice.

"I don't mean an *accident*," said Susie quickly. "I just meant that the old car broke down someplace and he is walking home."

"It may not be the newest car on this street," said Andy, unconsciously frowning at his sister, "but it runs better than some I could name. And if anybody should know, it ought to be me. I spent all last Saturday morning cleaning the spark plugs and draining the water from the fuel pump trap. And I even put in a new bolt that holds the battery, because the battery acid had eaten it almost through. If you want to know, our car gets better attention than almost anybody's you can name."

Susie paused to wink at her mother and make quick poking gestures toward the window before saying to Andy, "It may be just a woman's intuition, but I still think Papa's car broke down."

"Suppose you give your *woman's* intuition another crank," suggested Andy, "and tell me exactly what broke down. Was it the condenser in the ignition distributor or just some minor detail like the crankshaft breaking?"

Susie ignored these highly technical questions and said, "All I know is that Papa had to try several times to get the car started this morning."

Mrs. Carter lifted both hands in a pretending gesture of despair and said, "The only way to stop you two from arguing is to fill your mouths with food. We won't wait any longer for your father. Come!"

Susie was the first on her feet. She paused to look out the window again, then said triumphantly, "Just as I told you, here comes Papa, now—*walking!*"

She dashed to the front door, leaving Andy trying to remember the answer to a question that had just popped into his mind: *Did I or didn't I tighten the clamps on the starter battery terminals when I put the battery back in the car Saturday?*

"What happened to the car?" Susie was asking breathlessly.

"Never mind about the car," Andy heard his mother say. "Are *you* all right, Will?"

"Not a bruise anywhere except to my patience, Mother," said Mr. Carter reassuringly. "It was just the old car showing signs of old age. I got somebody clear over on the south side to give me a push to get started. Then it died, smack in the middle of Washington and Meridian streets, and a taxi gave me another push to get started again. But it finally died for good down the street. And there's where it is now."

"Well, at least it got you within two blocks of home," said Susie comfortingly.

"That doesn't solve tomorrow's problem," said Mr. Carter with a worried headshake. "The district supervisor is coming from Chicago on the morning train to help me close a big fire insurance policy. I've got to find some garage that will work on it tonight."

Andy walked over to his father and held out his hand. "Let me have the car keys, Dad. I'll run down there and take a look while there's still daylight."

"It acted to me as if the battery had gone completely dead," said his father, and handed over the car keys. "But I hope I don't have to buy a new battery *and* pay for a repair bill too—not this month, anyhow."

Andy started for the basement to get some tools, and his mother said, "If it isn't something you can fix right off, hurry back so your father can get on the telephone and find a garage that is still open."

Actually it only took Andy just long enough to lift the front-seat floor mat to find the trouble. It was what he expected. He remembered now that just as he had put the battery back into the car Saturday morning, and had tightened only one of the heavy starting wires, he had stopped to throw a few passes to Cornstalk Shaw, who had come by to show him his new football.

A couple of turns of a wrench was all that was needed. Andy turned on the ignition switch, stepped on the starter button—and the engine was running!

As he turned in the family driveway he tooted the horn twice as he passed the dining-room window, then put the car in the garage and came in to his dinner.

His father looked sheepishly at his mother and said, "I fussed and fumbled with that car for over an hour and almost got arrested for blocking traffic during the rush hour. But it only took a high school boy five minutes, all told, to fix it from the time he left the house until he was back again." He nodded across the table to Andy. "Thanks, Son. It would have been a serious matter not to have my car tomorrow morning when the supervisor arrived."

Susie gave her older brother a quick, sidelong, half-teasing, half-admiring smile. "If this gets around the neighborhood, *look out!* People will be calling you out of bed on c-c-o-o-l-d winter nights to get their cars started for them. And just think——"

Much to Andy's relief the telephone began ringing just then. Susie jumped up, saying, "It's probably for me, anyhow," and went out to answer the call. Meanwhile Andy had been wanting to say something to his father that he would almost rather lose his right arm than say in front of Susie.

He looked across the table at his father, then down at the fork in his hand, then back up at his father before he could get the words out. "I'm sorry, Dad, about the trouble you had with your car today. It was my

23

fault. I forgot to tighten one battery connection when I worked on the car Saturday."

"Lucky it didn't wait to go dead tomorrow, after my asking the district supervisor to come down all the way from Chicago," said his father unsmilingly. He gave Andy a serious look. "Closing that insurance contract tomorrow represents the biggest single commission I've ever had a chance to make. Remember, in business, Son, a man gets paid only for *good results,* not for excuses."

Andy's mother said diplomatically, "Perhaps it was the long drive we took Sunday afternoon over that rough road that shook something loose."

"I should have tightened the connection so it *couldn't* shake loose," said Andy, suddenly getting up from the table and going upstairs to his room.

Even though he had no written homework to turn in for the next day Andy opened his new advanced algebra book and with his elbows resting on his small study desk, which he had built as a sophomore in his woodworking course at Riverford High, he tried to dismiss from his mind what had happened that day. But the first chapter was just a review of his last year's mathematics course, so he skipped that chapter and turned to the next.

Immediately he ran into an equation that had him completely baffled. He was tempted to put his algebra book aside and pick up the latest issue of his amateur radio operator's magazine. In fact, he was actually reaching for the magazine when he slowly withdrew his hand and opened his algebra book again.

Andy knew he was not a brilliant mathematics

student. His average, though still in the upper half of his class, was only a "fat" B—but not quite a B plus, which would have put him in the upper third of his class. What Andy lacked in natural aptitude for mathematics he made up for by extra study. It wasn't that he liked to study, but somewhere inside he had a streak of what grownups sometimes mistook for stubbornness. It wasn't exactly that; it was really that Andy felt uncomfortable when someone else among his friends could do things in a way that made it look easy. Like the way Ken Blair threw long forward passes so casually that it looked as if anybody ought to be able to do it.

Andy was just finding out by rereading the first chapter of his new algebra course how to work that first equation in Chapter Two when his father came into the room and put his hand on his son's shoulder.

"I'm sorry if I said anything, Son, at the dinner table that hurt your feelings," said his father.

Andy shook his head slowly. "It wasn't anything you said, Dad. It was—well—I mean, I got to thinking about what happened at school today."

His father glanced at the half-solved equation on Andy's scratch-pad and smiled slowly. "By the looks of things you've already managed to get your mind off whatever unpleasant thing happened."

Andy rolled his pencil across his scratch-pad with the palm of his hand before saying, "Dad, I want to drop that two-period machine shop course and take something else instead. Mr. McCall, the principal, says I can do it if I get your written permission."

"Drop that machine shop course?" Andy's father gave his son a puzzled look. "Why, ever since you were in the sixth grade you've been talking about the time when you would be a senior in high school so you could take the machine shop course. What has changed your mind so suddenly?"

Andy rolled his pencil back down over his scratch-pad and said, "I can't remember the time, either, **Dad,** when I didn't want to be quarterback of the football team, and this season is my last chance." Then Andy went on to explain that the only machine shop class which did not conflict with his other courses came during the seventh and eighth periods. Then he added gloomily, "Our new coach told us, in so many words, that any boy who could not report every day for practice immediately after the close of the sixth class hour did not have a ghost of a chance to make the first-string varsity. That means Ken Blair, who is only a junior, will win his varsity letter again this year while I sit on the substitute bench."

Andy's father waited a long moment before asking, "Does that mean, Son, that a high school football letter means more to you than the *best possible* preparation you can get for studying engineering at college?"

"But I can take a machine shop course at college," argued Andy. "Plenty of fellows come from high schools that don't have a shop course and get their engineering degree just the same."

"I don't doubt it," admitted his father, reaching for his fountain pen and drawing a pad of blank theme paper toward him as he added, "but the more practical experience a young engineer has in how to make the things himself, with his own hands, the better engineer he will be when he designs things for others to make.

But if that's what you want, I'll give my written permission for you to drop your machine shop course so you can have a fair chance to win your football letter."

Andy's father wrote a brief note, signed it, and handed it to his son, adding quietly, "All I ask, Son, is that you talk this over with Mr. Stark, the machine shop teacher, before you make your final decision."

Andy flashed his father an enthusiastic smile. "Thanks a million, Dad. You're the swellest father I know."

Andy received a firm poke in the ribs from his father's thumb and, "I'm not too sure about that. It is up to you now to prove that you can make good grades *and* your football letter too. Don't let me down."

After his father had left the room, Andy reached up and took down a framed certificate from the wall back of his study desk that read, "Reserve Football Award. Issued to Andrew Carter for His Team Spirit and Faithful Attendance at All Football Practice."

Andy removed the certificate, then hung the empty frame back in its place—all ready to receive that coveted varsity block R that nothing in this world was going to stop him from getting now!

Chapter 3

On Tuesday, the first day of the fall term at Riverford High, curious Susie noticed that Andy's schoolbooks were stacked at his elbow and that he was keeping one eye on the clock as he ate his breakfast.

"Why the mad rush?" she asked. "It's more than an hour yet before the first-period bell rings. And I *know* you haven't any first-period class." She reached for a piece of toast and sighed. "When I get to be a senior I'm going to plan my last year's courses so I won't have to go to school before the *second* hour."

"Sorry, got to hurry," said Andy, gathering up his books and pushing back his empty cocoa cup. "I'll tell you all about it after football practice tonight." He glanced over at his father, saying seriously, "I haven't forgotten, Dad," and left the house.

"What is all this mystery?" Andy heard Susie asking as he closed the front door behind him and started for school at a dogtrot.

It was a mile from Andy's home to school. During the football season he usually jogged the full distance to keep in top physical condition. But this morning he had jogged only a half mile before he overtook Ted Hall, walking in the same direction.

Ted peered at him through his thick eyeglasses and asked, "Where's the fire or murder or what? Such haste is unseemly for a dignified senior."

"What are *you* doing, heading for school this early?" Andy countered.

"I have certain responsibilities as an executive," said Ted, and grinned to show that he was not taking himself seriously. "As student manager of the team I've got to get to the gym early and sort that mixed-up box of shoes into pairs for the reserve squad. Bad business having fellows running around in two left shoes or two right ones. People's feet don't usually grow that way."

Ted paused to give Andy another inquiring look. "That reminds me of something else that is part of my official business. Have you untangled your conflict in class hours so that you can keep those new varsity shoes I gave you, or will you have to turn them in and draw an old pair from the reserve box?"

Andy passed over the note which his father had written granting permission for him to drop the late-afternoon machine shop course and take a first-period course in its place.

Ted read the note, then handed it back, saying admiringly, "Anybody who can argue grownups around to his ideas the way you can, old horse, should try out for the debating team. You'd win in a breeze."

Andy said a little gloomily, "I don't think you read Dad's last sentence," then read it aloud for Ted's benefit: " 'However, I am leaving the final decision in this matter to my son.' "

"What are you crying about?" Ted asked brusquely. "You may not know it, because your folks are *different*. Most grownups do all the deciding and you have to do exactly as you're told. Here you've got a chance to do your own deciding and you put up a groan."

Andy folded the note and tucked it back into his shirt pocket with a little sigh. "This is one time I wish

Dad *had* done all the deciding. Now I've got to talk it all over again with Mr. Stark and convince him, too, that it is the right thing to drop the machine shop course he teaches."

"If you ask me," said Ted pointedly, "your big problem isn't talking this over with Mr. Stark. You can tell him that you have decided, with your father's permission, to drop machine shop and there's nothing he can do about it. I mean, you've got to *make* a place for yourself on the varsity first string this year. It's your last chance, remember."

"I'm going to feel like a chump if I don't," admitted Andy soberly.

Ted gave him an encouraging jab in the ribs with his thumb. "I don't see how you can miss. That pick-and-shovel job you worked at all summer has put you in better condition than any other fellow on the squad. Cheer up, they'll be calling you the iron horse of Riverford High before the season is over!"

They walked on toward school—still talking football, naturally. But now they were discussing the comparative strength of the other high school teams that Riverford High was scheduled to play, and what were the chances of "the team's"—Riverford's—winning the sectional championship. Which meant, of course, beating Mansfield High in the last game of the season.

"We've got at least an outside chance," insisted Ted. "In the first place, we've got twelve—count 'em, twelve —letter men from last year's squad. Remember Mansfield lost all but Reynolds in their backfield from graduation last June. Reynolds may be a little better safety man than Ken Blair of our team, but then Ken will have Marshall and Jim Eddins with him again this year to back up the line on defense. And you, of course," he added hastily, then gave Andy one of his heart-warming grins. "Is that going to be something to watch! Mansfield has never played against *you*. So by the time they think they have Ken under control, in comes the iron horse of Riverford————"

Ted broke off with one of his quick dramatic gestures and pointed toward the empty seats of the football field, which, at that moment, they were passing as they walked toward the gymnasium. "And right there is where it's going to happen!"

Andy thought of the last two years when he had sat on the substitute bench and watched with a sinking heart as Mansfield High won by top-heavy scores.

Ted shot him a quick look and said, grinning, "Never mind those wild predictions I made last year, and the year before that, *and* the year before that. I operate on the theory that if I keep on predicting long enough we're bound to win someday."

They had come to the crosswalk leading to the side entrance of the shop wing of the main school building. Andy turned off there to have a talk with Mr. Stark, the machine shop instructor, as he had promised his father he would. Ted turned off in the opposite direction and disappeared into the gymnasium.

Andy was about to put his hand on the latch of the shop entrance door when he heard someone say behind him, "Got a minute to spare, Carter?"

Andy turned to see Coach Dorman beckoning to him. Andy retraced his steps and said, "Yes, sir?" then waited, wondering what the coach wanted.

"Suppose we go into my office," suggested Coach Dorman, pleasantly. "I've got something on my desk that I would like to have your opinion about." He unlocked the small door to his private office in the corner of the big gymnasium building and motioned for Andy to enter first. "Take that chair beside my desk and make yourself comfortable while I dig out of the filing cabinet what I want to show you."

Andy could not help noticing how the new coach moved with the springy step of an athlete in perfect physical condition, and how sure and direct he was in using his hands. When he pulled out the drawer of the filing cabinet he did it quickly without jerking it. Then when he had found the papers he wanted he closed the drawer with a single push but without slamming it. And when he sat down at his battered old desk he did not slouch but sat upright.

Suddenly Andy found himself looking into a pair of steady but pleasant brown eyes—brown like his own—and Coach Dorman was saying, "Mr. Skiles, your former coach, was kind enough to leave me his notes concerning the players from last year's squad who would be coming back this year." He turned back several pages before looking again at Andy. "What I am going to read you about this player is confidential—just between the two of us, understand. After I have finished, I am going to ask you some questions about this player because I think you know him better than any of his other teammates."

Then the coach began reading from Mr. Skiles's old notes: " 'This boy reported for freshman football three years ago. He was eager to learn the fundamentals and attended practice faithfully. But although he was larger than some of the other freshmen he never was quite good enough to warrant giving him a freshman football numeral.' "

Coach Dorman paused and said to Andy, "Here is what Mr. Skiles says about him as a sophomore," and resumed reading: " 'In his second year I had hopes that this boy would find himself. He had grown taller and stronger, and his experience at first base on the freshman baseball team had improved his physical co-ordination. He did not drop a single ball thrown to him during the season and led the freshman team in batting. However, as a sophomore candidate for the football team he failed to meet my expectations.' "

Coach Dorman skipped the next paragraph, then resumed reading: " 'This boy reported for football as a junior this fall in better physical condition than any other candidate on the squad. He had practiced forward passing all summer; and when I held a forward-passing contest at the end of the first week of practice, he threw the ball ten yards farther than any of his teammates.' "

Andy found himself looking again into Coach Dorman's steady brown eyes, which this time seemed puzzled about something.

"Here's the part I don't quite understand," said the new coach. He laid aside Mr. Skiles's notes and leaned back in his chair with his large bronzed hands clasped across his belt line. " 'This boy, in my opinion, has the makings of a good football player—not a headline-grabbing star, you understand, but one of those iron horses that every coach builds a team around when he is lucky enough to find one.' "

33

Coach Dorman broke off and tapped the sheaf of notes on the desk with the back of his hand. "But Mr. Skiles reports that this boy—*who knew his football fundamentals perfectly*—just couldn't deliver under pressure in a game."

"I think I know why," said Andy slowly.

Coach Dorman leaned back in his chair and said, "I promise that anything you tell me about this boy will never be repeated. Now give it to me with the bark off straight, and don't pull your punches."

Andy took a long breath and said, "This boy was *afraid*—maybe yellow is a better word for it."

Coach Dorman shook his head. "That doesn't match up with my first impressions of this player. Give me some actual instances to back up your opinion."

Andy looked down at his hands, then back up again, straight into Coach Dorman's eyes. "It's like this, Coach. When he was carrying the ball and a tackler came at him he would ease up a little. Not enough for anybody on the side lines, even Mr. Skiles, to notice, but just enough to keep from getting a hard jolt. And he used to do the same thing when he blocked for another ball carrier. He would bowl over smaller boys than himself, but when he was up against a boy near his own size——"

"Stop right there," said Coach Dorman, raising his hand. "How do you know all this?"

"Because *I'm* the boy Mr. Skiles was talking about," said Andy.

Coach Dorman made a curt movement with his right hand. "Carter, you're badly mistaken about yourself. I've coached football at three different schools, but you're the first boy I ever interviewed who did not show

34

at least some signs of the jitters during my first interview with him."

The coach cracked his desk with the palm of his hand emphatically. "You're *not* one of those incurable flinchers, Carter! Get that through your head once and for all."

The coach lifted his hand in a way to indicate that the interview was over. Andy stood up and tucked his new algebra book under his arm and said quietly, "That is how I *used* to feel. But this summer, when I was working on a construction job, I found out that I was as strong as, or even stronger than, some grown men." He broke out in a slow grin. "They called me 'Kid' the first week; but after I climbed a rope hand over hand during one noon hour just to keep my forward-passing arm in good condition, they started calling me 'Tarzan.' "

"Watch out, or that tendency to flinch at the moment of impact will come back," was Coach Dorman's dry comment. "I thought *I* was something extra-fancy as a triple-threat back during my high school days. But I overlooked the fact that I was playing behind a line of rock-'em-sock-'em teammates and that our competition was below par.

"So, when I showed up at college with my scrapbook loaded with clippings from my county-seat newspaper, I thought I was headed for big time. They played freshmen in our conference those days, and I fully expected to go right on being the star of the game."

Coach Dorman paused to draw his hand across a smooth-shaven square jaw. "On my very first play in a college game I started out on an end sweep. I made just one yard before a big tackle and a bigger line backer nailed me between their shoulders and slammed me back three yards. When I got back in the huddle I bawled out my upper-class teammates for failing to block for me.

"I lasted just five more minutes in that game," continued the coach. "My teammates opened up big holes —big, wide holes that let the defensive linemen get a clear shot at me. In those five minutes I became an accomplished flincher . . . It wasn't until the last game of the season, in my junior year, that I got cured of flinching."

Coach Dorman suddenly pointed to a framed photograph on the wall, a picture of a white-haired, dignified old Negro. "Uncle Joel, the janitor of our gymnasium, is the man who cured me of flinching after the coaches had given me up in disgust. It was the last game of a tough season, and the first-, second-, and third-string quarterbacks were on the injured list. No one else knew all the plays, so the coach had no one but me to call on.

"Just the night before the game Uncle Joel called me to one side and said, 'Boy, I have been watching you every minute of every game you have been in. Now if you would only *pretend* like there was a hundred dollars lying out there on the ground back of the enemy's goal line and those other boys was trying to keep you from getting it, you would sure go places with a football!' "

Coach Dorman broke into a slow smile. "That did it . . . Not a sports writer in the business gave us an outside chance to win that game—especially with a weak sister like me in there as quarterback.

36

"Queer thing about that game," the coach continued in a reminiscent drawl, "I carried the ball only on the first and the last running plays of the game; I didn't throw a single pass, and I punted only three times. When I faced the team in the first huddle of the game I pointed toward the enemy's goal line and said, 'Uncle Joel says there is a hundred dollars lying loose on the ground down there. Let's go after it . . .' We went there on that very first play," added the coach.

"Was there *actually* a hundred dollars down there?" Andy blurted out.

"There was at least *eleven* hundred dollars down there," insisted Coach Dorman solemnly. "One hundred apiece for every man on the team. I mean, in *satisfaction,* you understand. What's more, we kept on 'collecting' all afternoon."

Coach Dorman glanced at his strap watch and became all business again. "Sorry that I've kept you here gabbing longer than I promised. I'll see you at practice tonight."

As the coach was reaching for the door to the athletic department property room, where Ted Hall was sorting football shoes, Andy took his father's note from his shirt pocket and said, "If you've got time, sir, I'd like you to read this."

"Your pet play that you dreamed up all by yourself, eh?" said Coach Dorman good-naturedly, and took the note. He read it, then glanced up with a puzzled look of inquiry. "Is this note to Mr. McCall, the principal, what you intended to show me?"

"Yes, sir," said Andy. "That's why I came to school early today. I mean, I promised my father that I'd talk it over with Mr. Stark before I dropped machine shop and took some one-hour subject in its place."

Coach Dorman handed back the note—almost as if it were burning his fingers, Andy thought, and said, "Sorry, old man, but it is an unbreakable rule with me as a coach never to discuss a boy's study schedule unless I am asked to do it by the head of the academic department. If you promised your father to talk this over with Mr. Stark, then keep your promise. But you'll have to excuse me."

It was one of the hardest things Andy could remember ever having to force himself to do. He looked squarely at his coach and said, "If I don't report for football practice with the others at the end of the sixth period, sir, it will be because I will be in the machine shop for the seventh and eighth."

Coach Dorman shook his head, said, "Sorry, no comment," and left Andy standing there with his father's note in his hand.

Chapter 4

Andy walked slowly from Coach Dorman's office to the shop wing of the main building of Riverford High. He went down the steps to the basement and opened the door of the machine shop.

But the thrill that he had been promising himself ever since he was a freshman, that when he was a senior he would be running all those fine machines and making things of metal himself, just didn't come.

He walked even more slowly the full length of the room to where Mr. Stark, the machine shop instructor, was working at his personal bench. On the wall over the bench was a row of cabinets with clear glass doors, displaying a sparkling assortment of split bamboo fishing rods and reels—all of which Mr. Stark had made himself by coming an hour early and working sometimes two and three hours after school in the evening.

Arranged on a large white cloth on the bench were the glittering parts of an almost finished fishing reel, and Mr. Stark was putting the finishing touches with a file on the S-shaped crank for it.

Mr. Stark's hair was snow white; there was a touch of gray in his closely clipped mustache, and he wore a pair of steel-rimmed glasses that had the upper half of the lenses cut away in such a manner that he could look over them when he dropped his chin.

Out of the corner of one eye Mr. Stark saw Andy come to a halt at his elbow. Out of the corner of the other he glanced up at the big clock on the wall. He rapped the edge of his file on a block of wood to clear the chips from it and said, *"Mmmm,* somebody is walking in his sleep. Otherwise he wouldn't be caught dead showing up at school twenty-five minutes before the first bell."

Mr. Stark made one more stroke with his file, then laid it aside and took the fishing-reel crank out of the copper jaws of the vise and held it in the palm of his hand for Andy to see. "Pretty as a spotted pup, isn't it?" he chuckled, then pretended to peer fiercely over his low-cut eyeglasses at Andy. "This is the kind of work you'll have to turn in if you want an A plus in machine shop, young fellow. And none of this slicking up your file scratches with a piece of emery cloth."

As though drawn by a magnet Andy felt his hand reaching out to take the fishing-reel crank from Mr. Stark's hand.

The little instructor snapped his fingers down over the part in his palm and stabbed Andy with a stern look. "You might just as well start learning now the first rule of a good mechanic—never touch another man's work or his tools. And remember that when you graduate from college and come strutting into a machine shop with your engineering degree still dripping wet ink. Nothing burns up a self-respecting mechanic like having the boss pawing over his tools and his work."

Andy got another crusty look, and Mr. Stark said, "Quit standing there as if you had a muskrat trap clamped over your mouth. Open up and tell me what's on your mind—football, I'll bet a hat."

Only freshmen were ever frightened—and then not for long—by the way Mr. Stark glowered and barked.

But more than one new teacher, overhearing the old shop instructor "practically eating a boy alive," had rushed in a high state of indignation to Mr. McCall.

Mr. McCall would listen to the complaint very patiently. Then he would say—without even a faint trace of a smile, "Strange as it may sound, there is no higher distinction a boy of this school can attain than to receive a complete dressing down by Mr. Stark. At the next dinner of the Alumni Association I suggest that you observe how many of the speakers attribute their success in later life to one of Mr. Stark's person-to-person lectures."

Which explains why Andy, who had just left Coach Dorman feeling as though the world were coming to an end, was grinning to himself as he took his father's note from his shirt pocket. But not for anything he could think of would he have allowed that grin to show, because that would have spoiled everything. Mr. Stark had no time to waste on a boy who wasn't at least smart enough to *pretend* that he was impressed.

Mr. Stark took the still folded note from Andy and grumbled, "Learn to *unfold* a document before you ask somebody else to waste his time reading it." And then he proceeded to read the note.

He handed it back to Andy and said, "This is addressed to Mr. McCall. If you have decided to drop machine shop in order to chase a football all afternoon, it is no concern of mine."

Andy said, "But I haven't decided *yet* that football comes first. I promised my father I'd talk it over with you first."

This seemed to annoy Mr. Stark more than anything

41

Andy had said so far. He frowned over his glasses and said, "So I am to be the goat in this matter, eh? I'm supposed to take the responsibility for deciding your future. Then if you make a mess of your life you can look back and say, 'It is all that windy fellow Stark's fault! Instead of grubbing away at this job of designing airplanes or diesel engines I might have been a famous football coach, with my name in the papers every day for two months in the fall'—and doctoring for nervous indigestion the rest of the year, no doubt." Mr. Stark tossed in that last remark free of charge and picked up his file again.

Andy just stood there saying nothing, for as every boy in school knew, or had been told by an older boy, the best way to keep Mr. Stark talking was to keep your mouth shut and wait until he actually ordered you out of his sight.

Mr. Stark put his file away in a drawer, brushed off the bench, and then carefully wrapped up the parts for his handmade fishing reel in that piece of clean white cloth. Then, without looking at Andy, he waved to a number of framed pictures of machinery that were hung on the walls of the room. "If you haven't anything else to do before the first bell rings, take a look at those pictures. Every one of those machines was designed by an engineer who passed through this machine shop course you're dropping. After you've looked 'em over, come back and tell me how many pictures of famous football coaches who started their careers here at Riverford are hanging in the Trophy Room of the gym."

Andy had seen most of those pictures before. But a new one—a large color photograph of a powerful diesel locomotive—had been hung since he saw them last. Across the lower right-hand corner of the photograph was written, "To the best engineer of us all, John Stark —from one of his many ardent admirers, Walter L. Cutting (Riverford '28)."

Pasted on the lower right-hand corner of the glass over the picture was a curt warning to the world, written in crabbed, square letters: "Warning! Never believe all you read. J.S."

The picture hung beside a window, through which could be seen the tracks of the Monon Railroad. And just as Andy had finished looking at the picture he heard the whistle of the Hoosier Limited, bound for Chicago. Then a big diesel locomotive flashed by—a duplicate of the one in the picture that he had just been looking at!

There were still five minutes left before the first bell would ring. Unaware that Mr. Stark, across the room, was watching him closely, Andy lifted his sagging shoulders and headed straight for the property room of the gym. Mr. Stark drew his hand across his bristly gray mustache and indulged in a silent chuckle of triumph.

Scarcely a minute later Andy had taken the new pair of football shoes, which Ted Hall had given him yesterday, from his locker and dropped them on the floor beside Ted, who had just finished sorting the box of old shoes for the reserve squad.

"For Pete's sake, don't tell me now they don't fit," said Ted wearily. "They just got to fit, because Coach Dorman says there isn't another dime in the athletic department budget for more shoes. That's why the reserves are wearing these old ones from last year's varsity."

"Give these to Cornstalk," said Andy. "I noticed yesterday that he was wearing old ones that made him stumble when he tried to catch a long pass."

Ted straightened up with a jerk. "You mean——" But he saw the answer in Andy's nod even before he got the question out, and groaned, *"No!* You can't quit football, Andy. You just *can't.* Why, this is the first year we've had even a chance to beat Mansfield. But it is going to take manpower, and plenty of it, to do it." He grabbed Andy's arm and shook it. "Look—it's the fourth quarter, with just six minutes left. We've just come from behind to score a touchdown, but we miss the try for the extra point. Mansfield leads us 7 to 6——"

Carried away by his imagination, Ted pointed with his free hand at the row of shower bath stalls as though they were the gridiron. "Ken has just carried the ball down to Mansfield's thirty-yard line. But he doesn't get up after he's tackled. You know what that means when Ken isn't the first one up. He's hurt is why! Wants to stay in but can't."

Ted gave Andy's arm a frantic shake. "This is no spot to send in a green sophomore substitute. It has to be *you.* Now get in there and *win* this game for us!"

"Take it easy," said Andy, nodding in the direction of the shower stalls. "That isn't a football field, and the game with Mansfield is almost two months from now."

"Oh, *rats!*" said Ted Hall, picking up Andy's new football shoes and cramming them back into the cardboard box in which they had come. "If you can't *feel* yourself playing in a football game before it happens you're hopeless. Go ahead; quit football then."

Andy's experiences with these occasional outbursts of disgust from his friend dated back to before they were old enough to go to school—back to the days even before Ted's parents realized that their son was seriously handicapped with nearsightedness. In fact, most of Andy's fights with other boys had been in defense of his clumsy but impetuous friend.

However—though he could not have said it in so many words—Andy did know that Ted never ranted at him for any selfish reason—never because Ted wanted something for himself. Ted's proddings and scoldings were always for the purpose of "firing up," as he put it, some other boy—principally Andy—who showed signs of giving up too easily. In other words, quitting was almost as disgraceful as lying or stealing, in Ted's eyes.

Andy gave Ted a steady look and said, "Now get this through your head, wild man. I'm not quitting football: football is quitting me. You know what Coach Dorman said about reporting for practice immediately after the sixth period. In practically so many words he said that you might just as well turn in your equipment if you reported late."

"Now let me tell *you* something," said Ted, and gave Andy a poke on the chest with his finger. "My father is a lawyer, and I've heard enough talk about 'loopholes' and 'interpretations' of even laws passed by Congress to know that neither you nor anybody else knows exactly what Coach Dorman meant when he said that."

Andy got another hard poke on the chest, by way of

added emphasis, and Ted went on, "As my father says, the only way to find out is to take the case to trial. Then if you put up a stiff enough front, my father says, seven times out of ten the other side will offer a compromise."

Andy got the shoe box jammed back into his hands. "Stick 'em back in your locker. Come out to practice *after* machine shop, and *make* Coach Dorman throw you off the squad, *if* he is that sort of a coach!"

Just then the bell for the first class hour rang. Andy snatched his advanced algebra book from the bench and dashed for the classroom clear at the other corner of the main building and up two flights of stairs.

Chapter 5

Andy got a sharp reminder of how much football really meant to him just a few minutes after the opening of the sixth period. Mr. Stark had given the new machine shop class his usual talk on safety. Then, as though that were all he were going to say about safety, he clamped a piece of what looked like sheet steel in his demonstration vise and picked up a file.

"Before any boy gets to use one of the power tools," said Mr. Stark, "he is going to have to prove to me that he can use a file properly."

Then, while he was still looking over the tops of his spectacles, he purposely made an awkward stroke with his file along the edge of the piece in his vise. The palm of his right hand struck the sharp corner of the piece of "steel."

Instantly a scarlet stain began spreading over Mr. Stark's hand. He grasped his right wrist with his left hand and said very disgustedly, "It looks as if all that talk I was making about keeping your attention on your work as the best way to avoid accidents was wasted."

Then with a perfectly straight face he gave the piece of sheet "steel" in his vise a poke with the end of his file. The piece bent far over, then flipped back, upright—it was sheet rubber! Mr. Stark opened his right hand, exposing a small medicine bottle in his palm, from which he had poured the red liquid which made the stain.

He waved curtly to the class. "Everybody back to his

47

assigned work place. Your first exercise will be filing a *straight* edge on the piece of sheet steel that you will find at your vise."

Andy's work place was in front of a window through which he could see the door to the gymnasium locker room. He clamped his filing exercise in his vise and made a careful stroke with his file. But before he made the second stroke, the locker-room door flew open and the football squad rushed out for practice.

For a long moment Andy stood there motionless— watching his old teammates coming out. Then he lowered his eyes and resumed his work.

What he did not see was Mr. Stark standing right behind him. Or that when his machine shop teacher turned away without speaking to him there was a mild twinkle in his eyes.

Three times that afternoon Andy thought he had filed a perfectly straight edge on his shop project. But each time Mr. Stark sighted along the edge and handed it back, saying, "Get that hump out of the middle."

On Andy's fourth attempt Mr. Stark squinted along the edge very critically, said "Mmmmm" in a skeptical tone, then tested it for trueness on a precision surface plate. He marked "A+" on Andy's work ticket and said, "Hustle back and get your bench cleaned up before the dismissal bell so you can skip over to the gym and get into your football rig."

Andy looked at his shop teacher and shook his head. "I am not on the squad any more, sir."

"You *were* when I talked to Mr. Ellerly at lunch," retorted Mr. Stark, and blinked in that way he had of putting you on notice there was to be no argument about it.

"But—but Mr. Ellerly is only my advanced algebra teacher," Andy blurted out. "Mr. Dorman is the football coach."

"Mr. Ellerly," snapped Mr. Stark, "is something else besides being *only* a math teacher, young man. He was also a backfield star in his college days. Also he is now assistant coach under Mr. Dorman . . . Now get that sick-lamb look off your face and let's see you play the kind of football I always thought you had in you!"

That afternoon—already more than an hour late for practice—Andy put on his football uniform as quickly as his hurrying fingers would permit. Then, as though trying to make up every possible second of lost time, he sprinted, all out, the two hundred yards from the locker-room door to the practice field.

Just as he reached the field, a high, beautiful spiral punt rose from the toe of Mr. Ellerly, Andy's algebra teacher, far downfield. It went soaring over the heads of two boys who were staring up at the ball in amazement.

A football in the air was a temptation Andy simply could not resist. He put on an extra burst of speed at the moment when he was already feeling short of breath from his long sprint. He caught it and, still on the dead run, swept his arm back and threw the ball back to Mr. Ellerly.

The moment the ball left his hand, Andy realized that it was possibly the longest pass that he had ever made, and that it was going to sail over the head of the kicker, the only man watching it, and strike in the middle of a group of players.

"Ball! Ball!" he yelled to warn his unsuspecting teammates.

Then, seeing that the ball had been overthrown, Mr. Ellerly ran backward, downfield. He leaped to make a one-handed catch and came walking toward Andy, carrying the football in one hand.

Mr. Ellerly said, "That was a whale of a pass, Carter. But rather a foolish thing to do, don't you think? I've seen some very serious injuries result from that sort of thing."

"Yes, sir," said Andy miserably.

Mr. Ellerly dropped the subject then and there. He motioned over his shoulder to the farther end of the field. "I've had a little talk about you with Mr. Dorman. He says that if you want to play football *hard* enough you can work out with the reserves under Mr. Winthrop."

"That's all I ask," Andy blurted out, "a chance to——"

Mr. Ellerly cut him off with an uplifted hand. "You'll have to excuse me, Carter. I'm supposed to be working with the varsity backfield. Coach Dorman is ready to give out the first new play. Good luck, fellow!"

As Andy trotted toward the reserve squad at the farther end of the field he met Cornstalk Shaw going in the opposite direction—to where Coach Dorman's whistle had summoned the varsity squad to assemble.

"Hey," yelled Cornstalk, pointing in the direction he was going, "not down there—over here!"

"I'll see you over there later," said Andy, and kept

on trotting. Mr. Winthrop, the reserve coach, had been vainly trying to explain to "Shorty" Jones, a sophomore reserve quarterback, how to handle the ball and then get out of the way of the ball carrier after it was handed to him.

Just as Andy pulled up, still breathing a little hard, Shorty made the same mistake again.

Mr. Winthrop said wearily, "You must learn to get your feet out of the path of the ball carrier or you'll trip him before he even gets to the line of scrimmage. That's just the same as the other team's having a tackler in your backfield."

He saw Andy for the first time and beckoned to him. "Step in here, Carter, and show Jones how to do it. . . . Feed the ball to Jenkins on a straight line buck."

Andy crouched down behind the center. He took the snapback, faked the ball to his left, then spun to the right to give it to Jenkins, a lumbering sophomore fullback.

But Jenkins stumbled and fell before he even had his hands on the ball.

"Try again, Jenkins," said Mr. Winthrop sadly. "Those were your own feet that tripped you that time."

Andy saw the look of humiliation in the boy's eyes and said in an undertone, "Come in stepping high next time. You're forgetting you've got on football shoes. The cleats are tripping you."

The next time Jenkins came roaring by, knees pumping high. Andy had barely enough time to pass him the ball and jump aside before the ball carrier was across the scrimmage line.

"That's more like it," said Mr. Winthrop, cracking

his hands together sharply. "Try it again. Now watch how this is done, Jones."

Twice more Andy demonstrated feeding the ball to the fullback. Then Mr. Winthrop said, "That's enough, Carter. . . . Jones, step in there and show what you've learned. Remember to get out of the way or Jenkins will be running up your back. Everybody hustle!"

As soon as Mr. Winthrop was satisfied with the way Jones was handling the ball as quarterback, he turned his attention to his other reserve backfield candidates. And again he called on Andy to demonstrate. . . . Again as soon as Andy had his backfield man working smoothly he was ordered to step aside for a sophomore.

At the end of practice for the day Mr. Winthrop blew his whistle, then barked briskly, "Once around the running track and to the showers. And *run!*"

Andy was about to join the other reserves when Mr. Winthrop caught his arm. "Not you; I want to talk with you."

For a moment Mr. Winthrop looked down, watching the toe of his right shoe as he kicked thoughtfully at a bare spot. Finally he said, "This isn't going to make you very happy, Carter. But if you're still the same boy I've known for three years you'll take it with your chin up."

Andy suddenly found himself looking into a pair of serious brown eyes, and Mr. Winthrop was saying, "You understand my position. It is my job as reserve coach to supply the varsity squad with a new crop of boys every fall who know their football fundamentals. That means, of course, that I have to spend most of my time on the sophomores."

"I think I understand, sir," said Andy soberly. "About

all a senior on the reserve squad is good for is to show the younger boys how to do it. I'm willing to do that, sir, if it will help make the team stronger."

"I'll try not to make it too humiliating," said Mr. Winthrop with the barest hint of a twinkle in his eye. "Friday we'll have our first practice scrimmage against the varsity. The first time we get the ball on offensive, I'll let you show me how much you can get out of that big boy Jenkins against Coach Dorman's line."

Chapter 6

Friday! Every afternoon all week Andy had been helping Mr. Winthrop teach the sophomore reserves what
to do with their feet, how to block for the ball carrier,
how to back up the line on defense . . . Now Andy was
sitting on the substitute bench watching the reserves line
up for a practice game with the varsity. All the coaches
were out on the field acting both as critics and officials.

Jenkins, the reserve fullback—to everyone's astonishment, including his own—got off a high-arching end-
over-end kick that Ken Blair, the varsity quarterback,
caught on the ten-yard line. He came straight up the
middle with it, deliberately drawing in the less experienced reserves so that he could cut sharply to the side
lines and then break into the clear.

Three reserve tacklers made futile lunges for Ken's
elusive legs. He side-stepped them easily and started his
angling slant for the side lines. Now two other varsity
men were running ahead of Ken—both good blockers
from last year's squad. The only reserve between them
and the goal line was Jenkins, the reserve fullback.

Andy watched with a sinking heart while the two
blockers bore down on Jenkins. But the big reserve
lowered his head and rammed into them in full stride.
All three went down, and Ken Blair tripped and fell
over the pile-up and rolled out of bounds at the thirty-
five-yard line.

Jenkins looked to the bench where Andy was sitting
and grinned, as much as to say, "How am I doing?"

then trotted to his position as the middle line backer.

The varsity line came briskly out of the huddle and got set for the snapback. Andy could tell where the play would go—right over Walker's right tackle position. He had never noticed Walker do this before—drop his right foot back just an inch or two in order to get more power into his charge.

Ken fed the ball to the varsity fullback, Eddins. . . . Sure enough, Walker blocked in, bowling over his less experienced reserve opponent and opening a big hole for Eddins.

But Eddins got no farther than the scrimmage line, because Jenkins, seeing that big hole, came roaring in and drove him back three yards.

It was all Andy could do to keep from cupping his hands to his mouth and yelling to Jenkins to watch out for a mouse-trap play next. But he restrained himself in time. Mr. Winthrop was out there, and in these squad practice games the coaches kept up a running fire of comment between plays.

Just at that moment Mr. Dorman, from his position as referee behind the varsity squad, clapped his hands sharply. "You varsity linemen, open those holes and keep 'em open!"

The varsity lined up for the next play. Ken Blair took a look over the defense before bending down behind his center.

With the snap of the ball that same big hole opened up in the wake of Walker's charge. Jenkins came roaring in as before. But this time he kept right on going until his own momentum—aided by a quick shoulder block from Ken Blair—sent him sprawling. Eddins plunged, unhindered, through that same hole to mid-field, where Shorty Jones, the reserve safety man, tackled him.

During a momentary lull in scrimmage, and while Mr. Ellery was pointing out to the varsity left halfback why he had missed his downfield block on Jones, the safety man, Mr. Winthrop walked to the side line. He gave Andy a searching look and said, "I didn't expect you here for another ten minutes. Did you cut your machine shop class?"

"No, sir," said Andy solemnly. "I finished my shop project early. So Mr. Stark sent me out here to inspect the scoreboard. He said if I thought it needed a new coat of paint to report to him Monday about it."

Mr. Winthrop said dryly, "That makes it legal as far as I am concerned," and walked back out on the field.

The varsity resumed its steady march downfield, using simple power plays through the line. It was ob-vious to Andy that Ken Blair could have scored easily with one of his rifle-shot forward passes any time he chose, because Cornstalk at right end was cutting down and behind the inexperienced reserve pass defenders on every play.

When the varsity did get down inside the reserves' twenty-yard line, Ken walked over to Coach Dorman and said something. But the coach shook his head and said "No" loud enough even for Andy to hear. "We've got to work on our ball handling and blocking for the game with Grant High next Friday."

A few plays later the varsity jammed over a touch-down, with Eddins crashing over behind Walker after Jenkins had been neatly mouse-trapped again.

Andy already had his helmet on before the varsity lined up to kick off to the reserves—ready to go in and take charge of the team at Mr. Winthrop's signal.

But the signal did not come until after Jones had been tackled by one of Cornstalk's deadly tackles on the reserves' own ten-yard line.

Then came Mr. Winthrop's signal! Andy sprinted out to him and asked, "What plays shall I run?"

"Line bucks—tackle slants—end runs—long passes—anything in the book," said Mr. Winthrop. "Mr. Dorman wants to see how the varsity works against a varied attack such as Grant High will throw at us."

Andy said doubtfully, "I don't think our ends have had enough experience to catch my long pass, sir."

"That doesn't make much difference," said Mr. Winthrop. "If we can get the ball and a receiver down *behind* the varsity backs, it will teach them a lesson, I hope, that they won't forget in the Grant game."

Andy ran back and faced his huddled reserves and announced their first offensive play—a mouse-trap play over left guard, the same one that had fooled Jenkins twice.

This brought a wail of protest from Andy's own left guard. "Try something else, Andy. I can't move that big ox Walker."

"You don't have to," snapped Andy. "Let him through and go downfield for another block." He turned to Jenkins. "Don't try to side-step Walker when he comes through at you. That's my job to get him out of your way."

The play worked even better than Andy had hoped. Walker's aggressive charge broke through the reserve line easily. But just as he was lunging for Jenkins, a smashing shoulder block from Andy sent him sprawling.

With a wild whoop of delight Jenkins burst through the line. Eddins, the varsity defensive fullback, hit him with a rousing tackle but bounced off. It was Cornstalk, in a desperate diving tackle, who stopped Jenkins after an eight-yard gain.

Cornstalk got up rubbing his shoulder and said dolefully to Andy, "Don't do that to me again. That big sophomore of yours is worse to tackle than a sack of horseshoes."

"Cheer up," said Andy, grinning. "I won't let him lay a hand on you next play."

"Watch those mouse-trap plays," Coach Dorman was barking at his varsity. "Get in there and show me some *real* defensive football!"

In the huddle Andy said to his reserves, "This is old Eighty-three—just inside Cornstalk. Jenkins carries and I take out Cornstalk. You other backs knock down anybody you see."

It was a direct pass back to Jenkins. Andy led the interference, apparently not seeing the crafty Cornstalk at all but keeping his eyes on the varsity's right line backer. Then at the last split-second he pivoted on his left foot and took Cornstalk out of the play. Jenkins made it a first down, with yards to spare.

Andy helped Cornstalk to his feet and said, "Just as I promised, I didn't let Jenkins touch you, even."

"But what a way to keep a promise to a pal," sighed Cornstalk, rubbing his side where Andy's shoulder pad had hit him. Then he broke out in one of his slow grins. "It was a beautiful block—I mean, *if I* were watching you lay it on somebody with the Grant team next Friday."

Coach Dorman was clapping his hands again. "Too many yards, too many yards! Tighten up that line and use your hands on defense. Fight off those blockers!"

In the next huddle Andy said to his right end, Brown, a slim sophomore who had shown flashing speed in track meets the previous spring, "Go down until you get behind their safety man. Then cut in and look up over your left shoulder for the ball. I'll try to have it waiting there for you."

The play started as a wide right-end sweep with Andy carrying the ball. The varsity, knowing that he was one of the fastest men on the field, raced to the side lines to tackle him. Even Ken Blair, the varsity safety man, started running in that direction. Then suddenly Ken had to whirl around in a frantic effort to overtake Brown, Andy's right end, who was sprinting down the side lines.

Just as the varsity defensive left end launched his tackle at Andy, Andy reversed his field and started running behind the line of scrimmage—back for mid-field. Then while still in full stride he whipped the ball downfield with all his strength.

The ball sped high over Ken Blair's head, straight for Andy's right end, Brown, who was standing motionless to receive it—and with a clear field to the varsity goal line behind him!

The yell of triumph from the reserve substitute bench ended abruptly. Disconsolately Brown picked up the ball he had dropped and walked back to the huddle with it.

"You would have to spoil a sure touchdown for us," said one of his teammates disgustedly.

Andy shot the offender a sharp look of disapproval; then turned to Brown. "You did a swell job of getting behind their safety men, fellow. Try catching the next one with your hands loose—like this." Andy flapped his wrist limply and grinned encouragingly at Brown. "They won't be expecting the same play again. So this time fake in quicker and then cut back for the side lines. Remember those loose hands——"

Again Andy streaked for the side line with the ball, and again he cut back toward mid-field. But this time Ken Blair and the other two varsity pass defenders refused to be decoyed out of position. Instead they converged on Brown—now cutting in sharply.

Then Andy came to a dead stop, settled his weight on his right foot, and let go with a pass for the side line—apparently far out of Brown's reach.

But as the ball left Andy's fingers, Brown cut back and put on a blazing burst of speed. He whirled in mid-air, reaching high with one hand, and came down, flat on his back—but with the ball clutched tightly in his hands!

Two plays later Andy sent Jenkins over the middle, into the end zone for a touchdown. Andy kicked the extra point.

Coach Dorman, who had offered no comment on the last four plays, put the ball down on the one-yard line and said to the varsity, "For that you're going to do it the hard way. Now let me see you make ninety-nine yards without giving up the ball!"

Andy was dropping back as defensive safety man

when Jones came running out onto the field and said, "Give me your helmet. Mr. Winthrop sent me in to replace you."

Andy ran off the field and took his seat on the reserve substitute bench. He picked up a handful of cinders from the running track and let them trickle through his fingers. It was too painful to watch what was going on out there on the field.

As though to avenge the humiliation he had received for being caught napping on those two long passes, Ken Blair was driving the varsity team savagely . . . Eddins was tearing holes through the middle of the tiring reserve line . . . Then Ken Blair was throwing jolting blocks for his two halfbacks—better and harder than Andy had ever seen him do it all last year in a big game . . . Then Ken topped it off with one of his explosions off tackle and a dazzling exhibition of broken-field running to score.

The reserves had the ball for just three plays after the kickoff. Jenkins got away a wobbling punt which Ken caught on the dead run—scoring without a reserve's laying a hand on him.

Coach Dorman tucked the football under his arm and said, "I'm calling a halt on scrimmage before some of the younger boys get hurt." He gave his heavier varsity squad a sparing nod of approval. "That is the kind of football it will take to stay on the same field with Grant next Friday. But look at you—puffing and heaving like a school of porpoises stranded on a sand dune in the Sahara Desert!"

The coach put his hand to the back of his head and looked his squad over. "I don't know whether this is going to do any good or not," he went on, "but I notice that a lot of you boys are riding automobiles, from not more than eight or ten blocks away, to school every day. You don't build strong ankles and legs that way, fellows."

He paused, and for the merest instant glanced toward Andy, then went on, "I won't mention any names, but there is one boy on the reserve squad that I see *running* past my house to school every day. I don't think I need to tell you boys on the varsity how hard he runs, blocks, and throws a football. You've had a sample of it this afternoon. That's all. Jog twice around the running track and then to the showers with you!"

"Same thing for you reserves," said Mr. Winthrop, and waved to the running track.

Andy was having trouble holding the slow pace at which the squad was jogging. Gradually he worked up into the varsity squad, where he fell into step with Ken Blair, who was sweating profusely in the warm September air and breathing a little hard.

"Those were a fancy pair of broken-field runs you made," said Andy. "I'd give anything to make my big feet do tricks like that."

Ken Blair flung back, "Save your breath for running home past Coach Dorman's house."

Andy's ears and the back of his neck suddenly grew warm. He was tempted to speed up his pace and leave the whole varsity squad puffing along behind. Instead he slowed down until Brown, the right end of the reserves, overtook him.

"How does Frog Fingers feel now?" asked Andy.

"That one-handed catch was something pretty to watch."

A grin twisted Brown's lips. "As if I'd just crawled out of a train wreck. Boy, that Eddins is hard to tackle! Worse than a runaway steam roller."

Later when they were in the locker room getting back into street clothes, Andy carefully avoided any contact with Ken Blair. For one thing, a senior did not force himself on a younger boy; that just wasn't done at Riverford High. Besides, Ken had a quick temper.

Andy was sure that he saw Ken leave for home while he was stooping over to tie his shoelace. But when he straightened up again, there was Ken—standing in front of him.

Ken said a little awkwardly, "When you've got the time, I'd like you to show me how you throw that running pass."

"Sure, at practice Monday," said Andy.

Ken turned abruptly and went out. Cornstalk Shaw, who had just taken his schoolbooks from his locker, gave Andy a slow look and drawled, "How do you like that? He wants to learn the one fancy stunt you got that Coach Dorman *might* have to call on you for to win a game."

"If a running pass wins a game for us, what difference who throws it?" retorted Andy.

"Look," said Cornstalk, pointing to his brand-new game uniform hanging in his locker, "if I weren't to get my share of the glory for all the banging around I take from you iron men in practice, anybody who wanted those glad rags could have them. I'd sit in the grandstand and eat peanuts!"

"You would—not!" said Andy, roughing up Cornstalk's carefully combed sandy hair. "You fake, you'd throw away your crutch to play in a game."

Cornstalk grinned brazenly back at Andy. "I still think it sounded better the way I said it."

Suddenly Cornstalk stopped clowning and gave Andy a look that only two close friends understand. "Andy, I'd give *anything*—and I think most of the other seniors on the team would, too—if you were the first-string quarterback of the varsity."

Andy shook his head. "It's no fun to have to admit it. Ken does more tricks with a football than I'll ever learn. Look at the way he went last year as just a sophomore —passed for six touchdowns and carried the ball over. himself, for three more. This year—with a year's experience behind him—he'll go like a house afire."

"You forget one thing," said Cornstalk, still looking steadily at Andy. "All those scores were made in just *three* games—*in the only three games we won last year.*"

Cornstalk let that sink in before adding, "Everybody on a team looks good when they're winning. But it takes an iron horse like you to steady down a team when the going is really tough." He gave Andy a reminding prod in the ribs with his thumb. "You don't have to take my word for it. Think back over the only games you got into last year as a substitute—that last one against Mansfield when we had blown up higher than a kite and Reynolds was passing us crazy. You came in at the fourth quarter. All of a sudden we started smearing Reynolds every time he got his hands on the ball. And why? For no other reason than that the team knew you were back there as safety man, and that any time the ball got across the scrimmage line you'd be there to stop a score."

"And don't forget," grinned Andy, prodding Cornstalk back, "who caught the passes for the only scoring we did against Mansfield—long, wobbly, desperation heaves that any one of Mansfield's three pass defenders should have intercepted but didn't."

"And no newspaper photographer around to take my picture!" sighed Cornstalk in a mock tone of great sorrow.

Chapter 7

Andy was more than usually quiet at the dinner table that evening after the varsity-reserve practice game.

Susie, impatient to know everything that went on, including particularly events at Riverford High, said, "How did Rocky Jenkins do against the varsity in the practice game this afternoon?"

Andy knew what was expected of him, and to avoid an endless series of leading questions on the same subject for the rest of the meal said, "Jenkins is getting the idea of how to use his power without falling over his own feet. If he keeps on improving, Coach Dorman will promote him to the varsity squad."

"Then I'll have to forgive him for not asking me to the party the *Goblins* staff is giving," sighed Susie charitably. "He's probably concentrating on football right now."

Immediately after leaving the table Andy went to his room to prepare his algebra homework. It was still taking him longer to do his algebra than it took the other members of the class.

So it was after nine o'clock before Andy put away his algebra book and picked up his amateur radio magazine. There was an article in it showing just how to build an inexpensive transmitter—something like the one he was going to build just as soon as he passed his amateur radio operator's examination in December. And by way of keeping in practice he put on the headphones of a small three-tube short-wave receiver which he had built in his spare time during the summer. He tuned in a "ham" amateur radio operator in California who was talking by "dits" and "dahs" with a neighboring ham— in Maine!

While this was going on, his father came quietly to Andy's room and from the doorway watched what was going on with a faintly puzzled look on his face.

When Andy looked up he said, "All through with your homework?"

"Just finished," said Andy, then took off his headphones and offered them to his father. "This is *good*. A ham up in Maine is telling a California ham about his four kids, but he doesn't know yet that his contact is an S.Y.L.—a girl operator!"

His father put one earphone to his ear and listened briefly, then handed it back. "Sounds like crickets chirping to me. Do you actually make sense of that racket, Son?"

"If they don't send faster than twelve words a minute, it's just as if they were talking, almost," said Andy.

His father nodded down at the radio magazine in Andy's lap. "Can you listen to that cricket chorus and understand what you're reading—both at the same time?"

A blank look came over Andy's face for a moment. He smiled sheepishly. "I never thought of it that way before. But I guess I do, because I remember what I was reading while those two radio hams were talking."

His father gave Andy a light tap on the point of his shoulder with the back of his fingers and said, "Don't stay up too late doing that double reading-and-listening act, Son. Your mother thought you looked pretty tired out at the dinner table tonight. A little too much football on top of a full schedule at school, she thought."

Andy looked up at his father. "I played less than four minutes of the game, Dad. I wasn't tired, I was just thinking things out."

"Maybe a little sorry that you didn't drop your machine shop course so you could play on the varsity?" suggested his father quietly.

"No, *sir!*" said Andy instantly. "Why, just today Mr. Stark told me that whenever I finished my class project ahead of time, and he could give me an A grade on it, I could make some of the special parts and fittings for the radio rig I'm going to build afternoons when the football season is over. And the best part of it is, Dad, he brought up the subject himself. I didn't drop a single hint." Andy broke out in a wide grin. "But that isn't saying I wasn't planning to ask him as soon as my first report card showed an A in machine shop!"

His father chuckled and said, "I never have figured out your system, Son. You seem to get more people to do what you want them to do *without your asking first* than any boy I know."

"My system doesn't seem to work on Coach Dorman," said Andy. He tried to say it carelessly, but there was a flat glumness in his tone.

"Never waste a good system on a bad prospect," said his father briskly. "If you're now sure that you haven't as good a chance as any other boy in school to win your varsity letter, I'd say drop football and put in that time on radio. You'll get more fun and less bruises out of it. Besides, it will be valuable experience for you as an engineer."

"It isn't as easy as that," said Andy, looking down at his hands. "The reason I didn't win my letter in my sophomore and junior years—well, I was always just a little bit scared. I don't mean afraid, you understand, of getting hurt. But—well, I just didn't know how much fun there is in making a hard tackle or running right through a big fellow's arms when I was carrying the ball."

"*Mmmm,*" said his father, stroking his chin, "this thing is getting complicated. What happens when you run into a big fellow and he slams you down good and hard?"

Andy broke out in a grin. "I just found out today. It doesn't hurt any more than if you had eased up just a little bit before he tackled you."

"And then you see a flock of stars," his father said.

"And then you get up feeling good inside because you aren't scared any more," said Andy soberly. "I can't explain it, Dad. But even playing as a *substitute* 'way down on the reserve squad is more fun than I ever had when I was practicing with the varsity."

His father gave Andy another one of those friendly taps on the shoulder with the back of his fingers. "Don't worry too much about explaining things like that, even to yourself. Everybody has thoughts he can't put into words that anybody else would understand. Good night, Son."

After his father had left the room, Andy put on his headphones again and picked up his radio magazine. He had lost his place, but that did not matter because he had found another interesting article. This one was about how to build a two-way communicating system by which his mother could talk to anybody who rang the front door bell without leaving the kitchen and that person could talk back to her. The best part of it was that he had, down in the basement, enough second-hand radio parts to build it.

While he was taking notes from the article for the parts he would need, two amateur radio operators were discussing, in code, some trouble one of them was having with his transmitter. This was something too interesting to miss. Andy put down his magazine and listened while the "doctor" was prescribing for his "patient":
$\cdots$ (S) $---$ (O) $\cdot\cdot-$ (U) $-\cdot$ (N) $-\cdot\cdot$ (D) $\cdots$ (S)
$\cdot-\cdot\cdot$ (L) $\cdot\cdot$ (I) $-\cdot-$ (K) $\cdot$ (E) $\cdot-$ (A) $-\cdot\cdot\cdot$ (B) $\cdot-$ (A)
$-\cdot\cdot$ (D) $--\cdot$ (G) $\cdot-\cdot$ (R) $---$ (O) $\cdot\cdot-$ (U) $-\cdot$ (N)
$-\cdot\cdot$ (D) $-$ (T) $---$ (O) $--$ (M) $\cdot$ (E), which, to Andy, meant, "Sounds like a bad ground to me."

After a short silence Andy heard the "patient" asking in code, "How do I sound now, Doc, since tightening that ground connection?" And the "doctor" answered, "O.K., O.K. Fine business, old man. I am copying you, solid, now."

"And me, too," said Andy without realizing that he was saying it out loud, and took off his headphones.

He picked up a newspaper clipping that had fallen from his study table. It was a picture of Riverford High's new coach, Mr. Dorman.

"New Riverford coach stresses balanced team play," the lines under the picture said. . . . A little farther down it quoted Coach Dorman directly. "But that does not mean that any boy with a single special talent will be neglected. Maybe a boy is only good at throwing one particular pass, or has an accurate toe for kicking points after touchdown, or maybe he is only good as a defensive player. That boy may sit on the substitute bench for game after game, but sooner or later he will get his chance."

Andy tucked the clipping under the edge of his study-table blotter. Somehow it didn't give him the thrill it had when he first read it in last Sunday's paper—especially since Tuesday morning before school, when he had tried to explain things to Coach Dorman, who hadn't seemed to understand what he was trying to say. . . . Then after Andy was in bed and the room was dark he wished that Coach Dorman could tune in on his wave length the way Dad could. . . . All you had to do in talking to Dad was get somewhere near the idea and he gave you that little bat against the shoulder with the back of his hand—sort of code for saying, "O.K., O.K., old man. Fine business. I am copying you, solid. . . ." By then Andy was alseep.

Chapter 8

On Monday afternoon of the second week of school as Andy put on his practice uniform in the deserted locker room he felt more like taking part in a rousing scrimmage than ever before. For one thing he wanted to test himself—to be sure that the way he had played Friday in that short practice game was no mere accident. He wanted to be sure that, *even if he never played in a regular game with the varsity,* football was going to be fun from now on.

The moment he stepped outside and felt his cleats crunch into the cinders of the path leading to the practice field Andy broke into a warm-up run. He was running harder when he passed a group of the varsity men who were practicing long forward passes.

Suddenly he heard Ken Blair yell, "Hey, Andy, come back here!"

Without breaking his stride Andy cut sharply to his right and circled back. He turned that way for practice because he was trying to break himself of the habit of always turning to the left when he was dodging a tackler.

"What's on your mind?" he asked, coming to a quick stop in front of Ken, who was holding a football.

Ken flipped the ball to him, saying, "You promised Friday to show me that running-pass stunt," then added impatiently, "I can't get 'em off for distance the way you seem to do. Which foot is on the ground when you throw it?"

Andy rolled the ball over in his hands and frowned thoughtfully at it and said, "I don't remember. I just heave it when it feels right."

"Then throw one and I'll watch how you do it," said Ken. "And hurry, because Coach Dorman will be calling us in for signal drill in a minute."

Andy looked around for Cornstalk to act as his pass receiver. He didn't have to look far because Cornstalk was standing not ten feet away and looking straight at him and making no attempt to conceal how he felt about Ken's abrupt manner of demanding a favor instead of asking decently for it.

"Straight down thirty yards, then cut to the middle," said Andy to Cornstalk. He flipped the ball to a varsity substitute center and rested his hands on his knees, waiting for the snapback.

"I'll run right beside you and watch," said Ken.

The ball came back. Andy ran parallel to an imaginary scrimmage line, keeping track of Cornstalk's downfield progress out of the corner of his eye. Then he whirled and ran back toward his right. When he saw his receiver was about ready to break for the middle he threw the ball without stopping to think which foot was on the ground.

He got the distance he was trying for, but he had underestimated Cornstalk's uncanny speed in breaking to the left. The ball flashed behind his receiver and struck the turf.

"Never mind the accuracy," said Ken. "I see how you do it now. I'll try the next one."

Without waiting for Cornstalk to retrieve the missed ball and return to the scrimmage line Ken picked out another end for his receiver. "Go down a little farther than Cornstalk did before you cut in," he directed, and got set for the pass.

He executed the play perfectly—leading his end just enough so that the ball hit the outstretched hands of the receiver.

Just then Mr. Ellerly walked up and said, "Let's see you pull that neat stunt again, Blair."

Ken repeated the pass play with still another end.

"Looks good," said Mr. Ellerly. "With a little polishing I think we can surprise Grant with that one Friday."

"That one is the Carter Special Delivery," drawled Cornstalk loud enough, at least, for Andy to hear—and Mr. Ellerly would have had to have been thinking about something else if he had not heard too.

But all Mr. Ellerly said was, "You varsity men get back upfield. Mr. Dorman is ready to explain some new plays that we are testing on the reserves tonight," and walked away without speaking to Andy.

When Andy finally arrived at the far end of the field, where the reserve squad was going through signal drill, Mr. Winthrop, the reserve coach, said, "What were you fooling around up there for?"

Andy smiled to himself but kept a respectful look on his face and said, "I was showing the big boys how that pass Brown caught for us Friday works."

Mr. Winthrop smiled guardedly. "I remember that one. Mr. Dorman asked me for a diagram of it after practice. He said he might even put you and Brown in the Grant game to work it if we needed another touchdown to win."

"I hope he does," Andy blurted out. "Brown is faster

than greased lightning—faster than Cornstalk—and the Grant team will be watching him all day. With a little more practice in keeping his hands and wrists limp until he has the ball under control, I think Brown can do it."

"Don't count on it," said Mr. Winthrop, shaking his head. "I think Mr. Dorman will save that play for a critical game at the end of the season—with Mansfield, more than likely. If we win that one, it will be a good season for us no matter how many games we lose."

Shortly after that Coach Dorman called the reserves to the other end of the field for scrimmage with the varsity.

"These are mostly pass plays," he said to Mr. Winthrop. "I'd like you to put in your best pass defenders."

Without hesitation Mr. Winthrop turned and nodded to Andy, saying, "You in at safety," and then named the other pass defenders.

From far back in his safety position Andy watched, with his hands relaxed on his hip pads, the first pass play developing. It was a skillfully executed rifle-shot pass from Ken Blair to Cornstalk, who had cut in just back of the line of scrimmage.

Up went Cornstalk into the air and took the pass, running. He feinted the reserve fullback completely off balance, avoided both defensive halfbacks simply by turning on a burst of speed and racing on toward the goal line.

Andy waited until he had Cornstalk trapped between himself and the side line before he cut down his man with a jolting tackle.

Cornstalk frowned disapprovingly. "I'll tell my

mother on you if you do that again," he drawled.

Andy grinned and gave Cornstalk a fatherly pat on the shoulder. "Bring your mother along next time, Sonny. She'll be proud of her little man."

"Just wait, you big steam fitter," drawled Cornstalk, and raced back to the scrimmage line.

Mr. Winthrop walked back to Andy, shaking his head and saying, "Too many yards. Too many yards. The instant you see that ball in the air, go for the receiver. If you can't bat the ball away from him, at least tackle him the moment he catches it."

Without stopping to realize that he was talking back to a coach, Andy blurted out, "You can't stop Cornstalk that way. You've got to tackle him from an angle or he will dodge you every time."

"You had that alibi last year, and the year before that," said Mr. Winthrop curtly. "Get over that bad habit of hesitating while you work up enough courage to make a tackle."

The shock of that last sentence was like a blow in the face to Andy. Mr. Winthrop must have realized it, too, because he added quickly, "It was the best tackle I've ever seen you make, at that. Make them sooner is what I meant to say."

On the next play—another pass—Cornstalk came galloping down the side line flapping his right hand high over his head and looking back over his shoulder. The two varsity halfbacks cut in toward the middle while fullback Eddins and Arnold, the other varsity end, ran shoulder to shoulder down the side line to Andy's right.

Andy had seen Ken score with this play too often to

hesitate any longer. The ball would go to either Eddins or Arnold, and the other would become the downfield blocker. But you had to watch out for a lateral pass at the very moment when you had left your feet for the tackle.

Just to be sure, Andy looked back to Ken. The varsity quarterback had his arm cocked for the pass, aimed right at Cornstalk, who had slowed down and was looking back expectantly. That was the giveaway for Andy. Ken was too smart a passer to look directly at his target.

Andy thought he saw Ken throw the ball, cross field toward Eddins and Arnold, and he was off running—this time for an interception, if possible. But he had taken just one stride in that direction when Cornstalk suddenly quit loafing and began running—still down the side line—all out.

Too late Andy saw the ball in the air—headed straight for Cornstalk. He whirled in desperation to cover Cornstalk but slipped and fell flat on his chest. Cornstalk pulled in the pass and trotted casually over the goal line with the ball.

Then as Cornstalk came trotting back he grinned at Andy and lisped, "My mamma told me to run away from you great big boyth when you tried to bump into me!"

"After this," Andy growled, "I wouldn't leave a burned-out radio tube lying around where you could get your hands on it, you robber."

Andy dropped back into his safety position again, too disgusted with himself to give proper attention to what was going on up there at the scrimmage line . . . It was another pass, of course. Ken was dancing around dodging reserve linemen and coolly waiting for a receiver to break into the clear.

"Look out for another long pass!" Mr. Winthrop yelled through his cupped hands at his pass defenders.

By that time three pass receivers were coming down the middle, not ten yards away from Andy. And the ball was in the air, headed for them.

Andy felt his cleats bite into the turf as he put every ounce of leg drive he had into the race for the ball. He raced between Eddins and Arnold and swept past Cornstalk, waiting with his hands outstretched.

It was like picking a ripe apple out of the lowest branch in the orchard, the way Andy felt when he intercepted that pass and went sprinting upfield with it.

Brown, the reserve right end who had charged in on Ken to break up the pass, suddenly whirled and threw a perfect block on him, the only varsity player in position to tackle Andy.

But as Andy broke into the clear, Coach Dorman sounded his whistle in sharp, commanding toots. "That's far enough, Carter. Throw me the ball."

As Andy trotted back to the reserve side of the line, Cornstalk shook his head and drawled sadly, "and he had such nice honest parents, too!"

That evening Andy came down to dinner whistling. His father smiled at him and said, "That sounds as if you and football were getting along better, better than usual."

"Not too badly," said Andy, smiling a little. "Any time you can steal a football from Cornstalk, it's a pretty fair day."

"You *stole* a football?" inquired his mother incredulously.

Andy didn't mind explaining what he meant. He felt as if he were reliving the satisfying moment when he held the ball in his hands.

His father was carrying on a conversation—listening would be a better term for it—over the telephone in the hall when Andy went upstairs to his room. He disconnected his headphones from his short-wave radio receiver and plugged them into a small code practice oscillator.

He was sitting at his study table tapping out numbers in international code and trying to make five smooth *dits* for the number 5 when his father came in.

Mr. Carter wore a slightly bored look. Andy removed his headphones to ask, "Can they hear this downstairs?"

"*I* didn't, at least," said his father. "I was listening to a long-winded father complaining that his son Stanley isn't being treated right by the new football coach at school."

Andy said, "Probably the same story Stan told me in chemistry lab and then tried to tell me all over again at lunch period. Everybody picks on Stan, according to Stan. He was moaning the same tune about Mr. Skiles, our coach last year. Nobody listens any more."

"I'm afraid my case is a little different," said his father ruefully. "It happens that Stan's father placed a nice fat fire insurance policy with me last month and is figuring on more coverage for his other plant in Batesville." He paused to give Andy a meaningful look. "In other words, I can't very well avoid asking you the same questions Stan's father has asked me about the coaching situation at school."

"If Stan's father wants the truth," said Andy, "tell him that his son gets the same treatment as the rest of us. Stan's trouble is that he expects more." He shrugged. "Maybe I would, too, if my father owned two furniture factories and was a director of the bank and I had a new car of my own."

"I'd hardly care to state the case that way to Stan's father," remarked Mr. Carter, looking sidelong at his son. "The way I get it, this is more like favoritism in reverse. Stan—according to his father—seems to feel that your head coach criticizes his mistakes but never gives him credit when he does a thing properly."

Without hesitating Andy said, "Our coaches don't just *criticize;* they tell you what you did wrong, then show you how to do it right. And that doesn't leave them much time to pat you on the back for doing what you are supposed to do."

"But Stan's father says there is *one* boy the coach never criticizes, even when he makes a bad mistake," said his father. "This boy is the star of the team, I understand."

"He means Ken Blair, the varsity quarterback," said Andy. "But that is a special case."

"I can't quite see the difference," mused his father. "If the coaches don't criticize this boy Ken the way they do Stan and you and the rest, then it looks like favoritism to me."

"It's got to be that way, Dad," said Andy. "Ken is the quarterback. He runs the team and calls the plays. He's the *boss* out there on the field during a game. If the coach criticized him in front of the rest of the squad, they would lose confidence in him. And believe me, Dad, when a team loses confidence in its quarterback, it is whipped right then."

Andy broke out in one of his slow grins at the somewhat baffled expression on his father's face. "Don't worry. Ken gets criticized. But it is always in Coach Dorman's office with the door bolted from the inside. And he gets criticized for all his mistakes, and all the team makes, in the bargain."

Mr. Carter rubbed his hand along his chin and said, "This throws a different light on the matter for me. I have a feeling that Stan's father, as a boss himself, as you put it, will understand, too."

Something in his father's tone made Andy look up quickly. "Dad, you weren't thinking that I haven't been getting a fair deal, were you?"

"As a matter of fact," admitted his father, "I have been strongly tempted several times to talk this matter over with your principal, Mr. McCall." He gave Andy a tap on the shoulder with the back of his fingers and smiled reassuringly. "I'm glad now that I didn't make that blunder. Better get at your homework now, Son."

Andy pushed aside his code practice oscillator and opened his algebra book to the chapter on quadratic equations in two unknowns.

Chapter 9

Right after algebra class the morning following his talk with his father about Stan and the coaches, Andy was seated in the library, where he was spending his second-hour study period reviewing his chemistry homework assignment. Next to mechanical drawing and shop, he had already decided that chemistry was going to be interesting—the most interesting, in fact, of his "book" courses.

He was also beginning to realize that his advanced algebra was helping him to understand chemical equations, because, just as in algebra, the symbols on both sides of a chemical equation had to balance.

At the moment he was looking up the atomic weight of hydrogen to prove that he had written the chemical equation for water correctly, a freshman, acting as messenger for the school office, came in and handed a note to Miss Tate, the librarian.

Miss Tate wrote her initials on the note and brought it to Andy, saying, as she handed it to him, "You are to see Mr. Dorman in the gymnasium office right away. Have Mr. Dorman record on this pass the exact time you report and when he dismisses you, and then return it to me."

Without the faintest notion of what Coach Dorman wanted to see him about, Andy walked into the small gymnasium office and laid his pass on the desk.

The coach glanced up at the clock, wrote down the time on the pass, then pushed it aside and motioned for Andy to be seated in the chair beside his desk.

"Before we get down to brass tacks," said Coach Dorman, looking intently at Andy, "I want you to know that I haven't any use for what I call a football *politician*. I mean by that a member of the squad who goes crying to other people that he isn't getting fair treatment from his coach."

The coach slammed down his right hand. "Every squad, it seems, has a football politician on it. He's the guy who never takes his complaint to the coach; he always works on some person of influence—his father, the principal, a member of the school board who happens to be his uncle—or he just goes crying around school about it. Whatever his method, the football politician wants something from the coach that he hasn't earned. That sort of player doesn't get *ten seconds* of my sympathy."

Andy exchanged look for look with his coach but kept his lips tightly closed.

Suddenly Coach Dorman seemed to relax and said in a conversational tone, "I'd like to know something, Carter. Why do you keep turning out for the grind of practice with reserves when you know that you haven't an outside chance of winning a varsity letter?"

Andy had already thought this out and was ready with his answer. "Because I like any form of athletics, and because I like to help the younger boys, like Rocky Jenkins for instance, get a chance to play in a varsity game."

Thoughtfully Coach Dorman pushed Andy's study-hour pass just a little farther away from his elbow. "Carter, did you ever think seriously of making a career of coaching? I'm not urging this on you, you understand, but you do have certain aptitudes."

"I did, up to the end of last year," admitted Andy, looking down at his hands. "But now I know that it is going to be engineering. Besides"—he looked up and gave Coach Dorman a wry smile—"it's pretty late to be changing my mind again. Most coaches were high school stars—or at least they were letter men."

Coach Dorman nodded slowly. "The odds would be against you," he admitted, then leaned back in his chair, his elbows resting on its arms and his fingers loosely clasped. "There are things that you can get from the game of football even if you never become a star or a letter man that will be valuable to you as an engineer. Sticking at the job when the going is hard is one of them. But the most important is being the best scrub on the reserve team, so that when you become the star quarterback of a team of bridge builders, for instance, you'll know what to look for when you start picking your own team."

He paused to glance up at the clock, then wrote down the time on Andy's study-period pass and handed it back. "Now if you will excuse me, I'll shift into my gym clothes and get ready for my third-period physical education class."

All the way back to the library Andy wondered why Coach Dorman had sent for him. Then just before he entered the silent library with its walls lined with books and rows of heads bent over the reading tables, he looked again at the two time notations that Coach Dorman had made on his pass. At first he thought the coach had made a mistake in reading the time or else the gymnasium clock was wrong, because it showed that the coach had been talking to him for more than ten minutes!

Quickly he looked up at the library clock . . . No, the gym clock was right. *At least,* Andy told himself, *the coach doesn't think I am a football politician or I would have been out of there in ten seconds.*

He was still smiling to himself when he handed his pass back to Miss Tate, the librarian.

Miss Tate said, "I am glad it was a pleasant conference, Andrew. Some aren't, unfortunately."

Some of the mystery over that interview was cleared up during the lunch hour, when he and Ted Hall were sitting on the grass in the warm September sunshine.

Ted, who had his drawn-up knees clasped in his folded arms, glanced owlishly at Andy through his thick glasses and said, "Cornstalk and Walker, and just about every senior on the varsity, are feeling pretty bad over a mean trick they played on you after practice last night. But not me, I want you to know. I tried to head them off, but they did it anyhow."

Andy ran the palm of his hand down over the knee of his corduroy trousers, which were traditional for seniors at Riverford High, and said, "So they were the ones who hung that wet towel in my locker and made me go home in damp cords, eh?"

Ted shook his head dolefully. "Even if they had filled your pockets with pickled frogs from the zoology lab, it couldn't have been as bad as this. They all went in a body to Coach Dorman and practically demanded that you be put on the list of players who will dress for the game with Grant, Friday. They were going to explain to the coach they would feel better if they knew you were there to come into the game on pass defense even if you weren't needed. But Coach Dorman ordered them out of his office before they got that far."

Andy picked up a pebble and flipped it off his thumb at a blackbird on the lawn that was regarding him with a suspicious yellow eye. Then he said, "That's the surest way I know of making Coach Dorman think I'm a football politician."

Ted dropped one hand, startled, and peered at Andy. "That's the very expression Coach Dorman used—*football politician*. But how did you know—has he talked to you since then about it?"

"I had a ten-minute conference with Coach Dorman —at his invitation—the second period," said Andy. "And in the first three minutes he did a lot of talking about how he had no use for a football politician."

Ted said slowly, "How would you like to have my place as student manager of the varsity?"

"No, for two reasons, and only one of them is worth mentioning," said Andy, flipping another pebble off his thumb. "The varsity already has the best student manager since I can remember—*you!*"

"Well, I won't be after tonight," retorted Ted. "Be- cause I'm going to the coach, myself, about this business. He must have lost his brains——" Ted started to rise to his feet, saying, "There's still ten minutes until the next class bell——"

Andy reached out and clamped a hand down on Ted's shoulder, ramming him back to the turf again. "Get out of that suit of tin armor and cool off, you chump. I don't want you charging over to the gym and sticking a rusty spear into a friend of mine."

In the scuffle Ted lost his glasses. He recovered them and put them back on with a grunt of disgusted resignation. "All right, if you won't let your friends stand up for you, at least wear a door mat on your back for people to wipe their feet on."

Ted took three strides toward the school entrance, with all the outward appearance of walking out of Andy's life forever. Suddenly he turned and gestured commandingly to Andy. "Come on, get going, door mat! I've just remembered that the new wire-recording machine for the speech class has flunked out. I promised Mr. Trotter that I would ask you to look at it."

Andy was on his feet instantly, and followed Ted into the building and down the hall to the classroom.

"There it is—silent as a trombone in a pawn-shop window," said Ted, pointing to the voice-recording machine. "And locked in its mute interior is an immortal oration of mine that I want to hear played back."

Andy already had taken his scouting knife from his pocket and was opening the screw-driver blade—the same knife that Ted had given him on his fourteenth birthday—when Ted said a little doubtfully, "Maybe we ought to wait until Mr. Trotter comes——"

With a very businesslike manner Andy pulled the extension cord from the baseboard electrical outlet . . . He tightened one of the wires that had been pulled loose from its contact screw—and plugged it back into the baseboard outlet.

"Now try it," he said.

Ted flipped the playback switch and, with one elbow

resting on the table and his chin supported in his hand, began listening raptly to a reproduction of his own voice: "Our hallowed ramparts, O ye football warriors of Riverford! are threatened with invasion by the barbaric hordes from Grant High——"

Andy reached over and flipped off the power switch, saying in a tone of professional reproof, "Tell everybody not to yank on the extension cord next time," and walked out.

"Hey, you still got a couple of minutes to listen!" Ted called after him.

But Andy kept right on going—grinning to himself.

Even though the mid-September sun was beginning to cast long shadows from the trees bordering the practice field when Andy joined the reserve squad that afternoon, the day was still uncomfortably warm for football. The other reserves, who already had been practicing for an hour, were grimy with dust and their old practice jerseys were damp with perspiration. It was the sort of a day Andy would much rather have been doing what Mr. Stark said he was going to do as soon as the eighth period was over—drive out to White River and cast for bass with the new casting reel that he had just finished.

Mr. Winthrop mopped his forehead just as Andy trotted up, and said crossly to Brown, the reserve right end, "You haven't caught a pass all afternoon. Wake up and try it again."

Brown wiped the perspiration from his eyes on the forearm of his grimy jersey and walked dispiritedly back to his end position. Jones, the smallest boy on the squad, took the snapback from his center and darted back three yards and snapped a sharp pass to Brown. It was thrown accurately into Brown's hands—but bounced away, over his shoulder.

Mr. Winthrop wiped his forehead again with his handkerchief and turned to Andy. "Carter, go in there and show Brown that it is actually possible to catch a forward pass . . . And you, Brown, go downfield with the receiver and *watch* how it's done."

Andy took up his position on the line at Brown's left shoulder and gave him a wink. "You're going to take this one. When I yell *cut,* break in behind me and take it." He flapped his wrists limply at Brown. "Remember —loose wrists and frog fingers!"

Andy deliberately ran slower than he could, going downfield in order to keep from leaving Brown too far behind. When he glanced back and saw Shorty Jones set to pass he yelled *"Cut!"*

Brown, dog-tired, stumbled as he obeyed the order. He was still trying to recover his balance as the ball left Jones's hand.

"Frog fingers, remember—frog fingers!" Andy barked at him.

Just as the ball smacked into Brown's hands, he lost his balance completely and fell down. He rolled over and came to a stop on his knees with the ball still in his hands.

"That's doing it the hard way," said Andy, pointing down to the goal line over which Brown had fallen. "But that kind counts six points, same as any other good one."

"*Frog fingers*—it works!" gasped Brown in a tone of

delighted surprise. "And even when you're stumbling over your own big feet."

He got up and raced back to the scrimmage line, beating Andy by a full stride.

Mr. Winthrop gave Andy a look out of the corner of his eye and said, "That was a rather 'free translation' of my instructions, Carter," then looked the other way —but not in time to keep Andy from seeing the twinkle in his eye.

Not having been assigned to either the defensive or offensive teams of the reserve squad, Andy started to join three scrubs who were taking turns at centering and passing the ball in punting practice. . . . His turn to kick the ball had not come up yet before Mr. Winthrop called him back.

"Take Jones's place as offensive quarter and show him how to get out of the way after the ball is fed on a straight line buck," said Mr. Winthrop.

Shorty, who already had been knocked down three times in succession by collisions with his own fullback, picked himself up groggily for the fourth time and stepped aside for Andy.

Andy, pretending not to notice the discouraged look on Shorty's face, said to him, "Just watch my feet. If I do this right, I'll step back with my left foot first— like this. Then as I feed the ball I take a half step backward with my right. That pulls my left shoulder out of the way of the ball carrier."

After going through the maneuver in slow motion without the ball Andy demonstrated it again with an actual scrimmage play. He had not planned to carry the demonstration further than that; but when a defen sive guard broke through, he drove his left shoulder into the guard and took him out of the play.

Mr. Winthrop glanced at his watch and said, "There's just time left for Jones to try it a few times," and motioned for Andy to step aside. . . . Then, after the younger boy had executed the play three times without colliding with his ball carrier, Mr. Winthrop blew his whistle and waved the reserves to the showers. And in almost the same motion reached out and caught Andy's left arm. "I want to talk with you on the way in."

In silence they walked several paces together up the path toward the gymnasium. Andy was wondering what this was all about, because he could not remember Mr. Skiles, the old coach, or Mr. Winthrop, who had coached the reserves last year, too, ever walking to the gym after practice with just one boy. It did not occur to him that it was *not* because the coaches were grumpy and glad to get away from a crowd of noisy and often clumsy boys, but the real reason was that they were being careful not to show favoritism. But, whatever the reason, Andy could not help feeling just a little "important" walking in alone with Mr. Winthrop like this.

Finally Mr. Winthrop said thoughtfully, "I want you to listen carefully before you start jumping to a half-baked conclusion."

"Yes, sir," said Andy automatically.

"Mr. Ellerly," continued Mr. Winthrop, speaking slowly, "has been quite outspoken in urging Mr. Dorman to promote you to the varsity squad. Mr. Ellerly has used what I consider a very strong argument. He says that it would be good insurance to have a boy with a high scholastic standing, such as yours, ready to step into the shoes of any one of several varsity backfield boys whose grades are questionable and who may have to be dropped from the squad when the first report card comes out."

After a few more paces Mr. Winthrop went on in the same thoughtful tone, "Mr. Ellerly also likes your defensive play. He believes that you would develop into a reliable pass defender, with a little personal attention. To make it short, Mr. Ellerly has persuaded Mr. Dorman to promote you to the varsity even though you do not get in as much practice as the others on the squad."

Before he could check himself Andy blurted out, "I guess I've been all wrong about Mr. Ellery. In algebra class he takes a personal interest in you. But out on the practice field—well, he acts as if he were so busy that you would think he never saw you before in his life. That's how wrong I was about him."

In a tone that indicated that, as a member of the Riverford teaching staff, he was not going to make the unforgivable blunder of commenting on either the methods or the personality of a fellow teacher, Mr. Winthrop said, "Perhaps you have overlooked the fact that Mr. Ellerly has only twelve above-average students in his algebra class while on the football field he has thirty active boys to occupy his attention."

Andy did not suppose that he was expected to say anything further on the subject and kept walking until Mr. Winthrop began speaking again. "Now I come to the hard part. Please listen carefully and don't interrupt until I have finished. The reserve squad, as you know, always plays four games every season, as a sort of reward for the boys who haven't quite had enough experience to play in a regular game."

"Yes, sir," said Andy.

Mr. Winthrop did not seem to consider that an interruption and went on talking. "The head coach of Mansfield High has come to an agreement with Mr. Dorman that the annual reserve game between the two schools will be moved ahead two weeks. That means we shall play them on Thursday afternoon of *this* week. Which also means"—Mr. Winthrop glanced sidewise at Andy to be sure he was paying strict attention—"*that any boy who plays in this reserve game Thursday will not be eligible to play in the big varsity game against Grant the following day, Friday.* That is a rigid rule of the state high school athletic association, made to prevent older and more experienced boys from playing on both reserve and varsity teams. You understand that, of course."

"Yes, sir," said Andy, beginning to have an uneasy feeling that it would be a lot more fun to dress with the reserves for the B game with the Mansfield reserves. That way he was sure of getting to play at least a full quarter—and longer if the game were close . . . But if he moved up to the varsity he was almost certain to sit out the Grant game on the substitute bench, watching Ken Blair and his understudy, Stan Marshall, alternating at quarterback.

As though he had deliberately given Andy time to think the idea through before going on, Mr. Winthrop walked on another five paces before resuming. "I am going to ask you to make a very difficult choice. It would mean a great deal to the younger boys on the reserve squad if *you* were out there on the field at the opening kickoff to steady them down. They respect you; they look up to you more, perhaps, than you realize."

Mr. Winthrop suddenly reached out and gave Andy's arm a little squeeze. "Think it over tonight. If you come to me before school tomorrow morning and tell me that you would rather move up to the varsity squad than play in the B game Thursday, I won't think the worse of you. You've certainly earned your chance."

Andy flipped a pebble aside with his toe and said, "I guess I'm what the boys call a fish, but I'll start the B game against Mansfield."

Mr. Winthrop shook his head. "I'm not going to accept that as your final decision. Think it over tonight. Remember the school rule for awarding varsity letters. *A boy must play at least ten full quarters during the season to be considered for a letter.* And remember, too, that only eighteen football letters can be awarded."

Mr. Winthrop turned off the path and disappeared through the door of the coaches' dressing room.

Andy walked into the players' locker room to find Ted Hall, Walker, and Cornstalk at the squad bulletin board, on which had been posted a typewritten list of names.

"Hey, Andy, come here!" called Ted, who had remarkably alert vision in spite of thick glasses. "Look— your name is on here, and in the most important place, too."

Andy put a hand on the towel-draped bare shoulder of Cornstalk and read, "The following players will dress for the Grant game Friday afternoon." Ken Blair headed the list as captain and quarterback; then fol-

94

lowed the eight seniors, including Eddins, Walker, and Cornstalk.

Rocky Jenkins, the sophomore fullback, recently promoted from the reserves, came next to last—then, written in longhand, in ink, was Andy's name.

"What did I tell you?" said Ted, banging his hand on Andy's back and pointing to the last name on the list. "Right where it can't be missed."

"First, but only backward," said big Walker, grinning teasingly over his shoulder at Andy.

"Shut up, you muscle-bound mammoth," snapped Ted, tapping Andy's name with a finger of authority. *"That's* where the Chinese always put the most important name on the list. And there're *millions* more Chinese than all the people of the world who use the English system."

"Now tell us a bedtime story in Chinese, Professor," drawled Cornstalk, giving Andy a congratulatory nudge in the ribs with his elbow. "Nice going."

Meanwhile Andy had been reading a short paragraph under the list of names which read, "Any player on the above list who, *for some exceptional reason, will be unable to play Friday* should strike his name from the list and report immediately to me before leaving the gymnasium tonight."

Without hesitating Andy plucked a pencil from Ted's shirt pocket and drew a heavy line through his name.

There was a moment of silence; then Walker turned away, saying, "I'm taking my shower before the water gets cold."

Ted snatched back his pencil and walked to the other end of the locker room.

Cornstalk turned to Andy and drawled grimly, "I haven't been in a fist fight since I was in the eighth grade. But I am going to have one with anybody who says you're *afraid* to play in the Grant game even if I have to take on the whole squad two at a time."

"Thanks, Cornstalk," said Andy, giving his friend's shoulder a grateful squeeze. He lowered his tone. "I'll tell you why when there aren't so many ears around."

He walked to the farther end of the locker room, where the reserves—usually the noisiest of the entire squad—were glumly getting ready to take their showers after the varsity had theirs.

Brown looked up, dangling one football shoe by the laces, and said, "Congratulations, Andy. But we are sure going to miss you in the B game with Mansfield, Thursday afternoon."

"They are going to smear us all over the field," chimed in Shorty Jones dolefully.

Still standing in front of a discouraged circle of faces Andy grinned and said, "Throw away your crying towels. *We* are going to take that Mansfield B team!"

A delighted smile exploded over Jones's face. "You mean, you're going to play with us instead of with the varsity as Coach Dorman says on the list?"

The other reserves were still a little stunned by the good news when Walker came out of the showers with a damp towel wrapped around his hips. He bent a teasing look upon the reserves and said, "Now, children, you mustn't be afraid of that big Mansfield B team. Those boys put on their football shoes one at a time, just the way you little boys do."

Five reserves, clutching their begrimed football jerseys, leaped as one man upon the big senior. And, in spite of his struggles, gave him a thorough rubdown. They hustled him back to the shower room and pushed him through the door. From which strategic defense position Walker gave them a mock frown of reproof. "You naughty, naughty, rough boys. If you do that in the B game with Mansfield, the referee will penalize you fifteen yards for offensive use of the hands—and I mean *offensive*."

Slyly Walker pitched a wink at Andy, as though saying, "How's that for firing up a bunch of scared youngsters?" and went to take his second shower.

Andy suddenly remembered something. He walked the length of the locker room and rapped on the door leading to Coach Dorman's small office.

"Come in!" called the coach.

Coach Dorman was still dressed in gray flannel slacks and a sweat shirt when Andy walked in. The coach pushed aside a scratch-pad on which he had been making notes. Mr. Ellerly was standing with his back to Andy, adjusting the knot of his tie in front of a small mirror. Mr. Winthrop had just put on his jacket and was about to leave through the side door.

"What's on your mind, Carter?" asked Coach Dorman.

"I've just taken my name off the list on the bulletin board," said Andy.

"Well, I'll be——" Coach Dorman stopped short at the sight of the serious look in Andy's eyes. "Sorry, Son. What's your reason—serious illness in the family?"

Mr. Ellerly turned and stared at Andy in blank amazement.

Mr. Winthrop said with more than a hint of impatience, "I told you, Carter, that you were not to make that decision until tomorrow."

It was Coach Dorman's turn to look puzzled. He said—not looking at anyone in particular, "Something important is going on in the place that the athletic director hasn't heard about, it seems," and then looked to Andy for an explanation.

Andy motioned awkwardly over his shoulder. "I've decided to play with the reserves in the B game against the Mansfield reserves Thursday instead."

"*Why?*" demanded Coach Dorman.

Andy looked down at his hands and said, "I know this isn't going to sound right—it's going to sound like, well—the younger boys on the reserves were getting a little scared of what the Mansfield B team was going to do to them. I could see it at practice this afternoon." He looked up at Coach Dorman. "I thought maybe they would feel better if they knew that a senior was on the bench ready to help out if they got into trouble."

Mr. Winthrop reached out and opened the door to the locker room part way. Instantly the small office echoed to the shouting and chatter from the boys out there.

Coach Dorman was unable to keep from showing a tight smile when he said, "Apparently you told them the 'bad' news before you told me." He turned slowly to Mr. Ellerly, saying, "Maybe this isn't going to be a bad thing for the varsity. If that Mansfield B team whips Mr. Winthrop's boys unmercifully Thursday afternoon, it could very easily have a bad effect on the varsity squad psychologically."

Mr. Ellerly nodded in sober agreement. "I've already heard some of the varsity talking about how big those Grant boys are—especially their fullback, Wilson."

Coach Dorman waved his hand briefly to include both Andy and Mr. Winthrop. "It's up to the pair of you to get this season off to a flying start. If the reserves take that B game, I'll make it my business to win the Grant game."

Mr. Winthrop shrugged and said, "Grant is the weakest team on the schedule. If our varsity boys don't take that game they are in for a bad season, and so are we, the coaches."

"Grant isn't the pushover you may think," said Coach Dorman in a ruffled tone that Andy had never heard him use toward another member of the school faculty before. He made a little gesture of apology with his hand, and went on in a more pleasant tone, "I heard at the high school coaches' meeting last night that Grant has a surprise for the rest of us—a pair of ends. They are twin brothers who transferred as seniors from out of the state. From Ohio, I understand, where they were quite a sensation last year against pretty rugged competition."

A little embarrassed by all this, Andy said, "Excuse me," and left the office, and began pulling off his practice jersey as he walked toward his locker.

Andy was late getting home that evening. The family was already seated at the dinner table when he came down from his room, after spending a few minutes listening to learn if any amateur radio operators were "working" the forty-meter band.

"What's the weather going to be like tomorrow?" asked his father, because Andy usually came downstairs with some weather gossip that he had heard amateurs in neighboring states exchanging by means of their radio telegraph keys.

Andy shook his head. "Too much static. Couldn't copy anybody but a W9 station from right here in town."

"It all sounds like baby chickens peeping to me," said his mother. "I couldn't understand it in a thousand years."

Susie was waiting—not too patiently—to break a very important bit of news.

"Guess what I found out today!" she said excitedly. "This afternoon on my way home I stopped in Tillman's sporting goods store to see if they had my size gym shoes. Mr. Tillman was busy unwrapping a parcel post package that just came in.

"It was a gorgeous blue blanket with a large gold block R in the middle—Riverford's colors, blue and gold—and right away I thought it would be a perfectly beautiful Christmas present for——"

"——for Rocky Jenkins," said Andy teasingly.

"No, for my brother, Andrew Carter," retorted Susie sweetly. "So I asked Mr. Tillman the price. But he said it wasn't for sale. He said it had been ordered by the Riverford Alumni Association as a football award, and if they could raise the money they were going to give one to every player who wins a letter this year."

"I can see them doing it," said Andy skeptically. "Blankets like that cost a lot of money. Eighteen of them would just about break a good-sized bank."

Mrs. Carter turned to her husband and said, "Will, let's drive downtown after dinner and see this gorgeous blanket."

"Might not be a bad idea, Mother," said Mr. Carter, nodding.

"Now see here," said Andy in an alarmed tone, "don't go blowing a pile of money on any blanket for me as a Christmas present or for any other time."

"Do you mean to infer," inquired his father, leveling a somewhat offended frown across the table, "that I'm not good enough as a family provider to buy new blankets for this family?"

"But you *can't,* Dad." Andy spread his hands in a gesture of desperation. "You just *can't.* I'd never live it down if you went out and bought me a *football* blanket with the school's monogram on it. All the fellows would say I had *bought* my football letter because I wasn't good enough to *earn* it the way they did theirs."

"Of course you will earn your football letter," said his mother. "Susie says all the boys on the reserve squad think you're the best player in school."

Susie nodded confirmation of that across the table to her father. "Rocky Jenkins says Andy is a *demon* of a football player. He said he saw stars for five minutes after Andy tackled him once."

Andy suddenly folded his napkin and laid it on his plate, saying, "I guess I'm not hungry," and went up to his room.

His father followed immediately—and was the one who closed the door to Andy's room.

"It takes a hard knock to do a thing like this to you, Son," he said, cupping his hand over Andy's shoulder.

"If it was anything Mother or I said at the table—well, we'll never forgive ourselves."

Andy had trouble keeping his voice steady when he said, "That isn't what did it, Dad. You and Mother didn't know . . . It's because I blew my chances for a varsity letter today. And I suddenly felt sorry for myself."

"Everybody makes mistakes," said his father. "I hung on to a desk job for ten years after I knew that there was no future in it. I was *afraid* to take a chance and look for a better job. It wasn't until I was slapped in the face with the realization that you and Susie were going to be deprived of a college education that I cut loose from a steady job and a regular pay check and started selling fire insurance on straight commission."

"I'm just a fish," said Andy disconsolately, then blurted out the whole story about scratching his name off the varsity list. . . . "And now half the varsity thinks I'm *afraid* to play football against fellows my age and size is the reason why I choose to play with the reserves."

His father gave Andy's shoulder a comforting shake. "Then go into the B game with the reserves and *show* them you're not afraid!"

Andy could trust himself to look up at his father now. He shook his head. "That's the trouble, Dad. Some of those Mansfield boys are much lighter than I am. And they haven't been doing hard work all summer, as I have. I'm not bragging, Dad. I'm worried. I could almost *kill* a smaller boy if I tackled him as hard as I know I could."

His father tapped him against the shoulder with the

back of his hand. "*You* know that you're not afraid, and *I* know you're not afraid." Andy saw a little smile flicker in his father's eyes as he added, "Go easy with the smaller boys on the other team, but crack the ones your size good and hard!"

As his father turned to go back down to his interrupted dinner, Andy got up from his study table and said, "Wait a second, Dad. I'm going back down myself. I'm hungry enough to eat an old car battery."

Chapter 10

Thursday afternoon Andy hurried to his machine shop class in order to see Mr. Stark before any of the other boys arrived. He wanted to make sure that Mr. Winthrop had made the official arrangements for him to leave early so he could dress in time for the opening kickoff of the B game with the Mansfield High reserves.

Mr. Stark, who never seemed to be idle a moment, even between classes, was busy at one of the metal-working lathes making a repair bolt for the engineer of the school power plant.

"Well, what is it this time?" asked Mr. Stark without looking up.

Andy said, "Did Mr. Winthrop send through a note about me playing in the reserve game this afternoon?"

Still without looking up Mr. Stark said tartly, " '*Me playing*'—what kind of English is that for a senior to be using?"

"*My playing,*" said Andy, correcting himself lamely.

Mr. Stark started a second roughing cut on the large bolt he was making and checked the diameter with his calipers before saying, "Mr. Winthrop hasn't sent through any note. Furthermore," he added while watching a steel shaving curling up over the lathe-tool bit, "the whole school will be dismissed early tomorrow for the big game with Grant. Now here you come asking to get off early today, too."

"*Please,* Mr. Stark——" Andy got no further than

that. Mr. Stark shut off the power to his lathe and frowned over his cutaway spectacles.

"Now see here, young fellow, I seem to remember that you came to me at the start of this term with a lot of lofty notions about giving up football because you had decided this machine shop course was more important. You'll never get to first base as an engineer if you keep changing your mind every Thursday."

Andy was tempted to tell Mr. Stark that it was because he *had* chosen to take machine shop that he was playing in the reserve game instead of tomorrow in the big game. But somehow he could not say it, and turned away to get his work apron out of one of the numbered drawers in the workbench along the wall.

"Come back here!" said Mr. Stark, pointing with his finger to a spot on the floor immediately in front of him. "Hmmmm—a fine engineer you'll make if you go walking off with your tail dragging every time the boss doesn't grab the idea you're offering right out of your hand." He rubbed his bristly gray mustache with a forefinger and closed one eye, squinting at Andy through the other. "If your idea is as good as you think it is, you ought to be able to prove to your boss that he should grab it."

Mr. Stark picked up a pencil sketch of the repair part that he was making for the power plant engineer and handed it to Andy. "Does this give you any idea of what I am driving at?"

Andy was still puzzled until he read the note at the bottom of the sketch: "Please rush this stoker bolt. Boiler is shut down, and cold rainy weather is forecast for tomorrow."

A quick grin broke over Andy's face. He looked up at Mr. Stark and said, "I could finish making this part—all but chasing the thread, that is—while you were getting the rest of the class started on today's project."

"That's just what I planned having you do," said Mr. Stark, nodding shortly. "Get at it. And as soon as you finish your part of the job, scoot for the gymnasium. But keep your mind on this job until you've done it right . . . Remember, though, if you spoil it you'll have to start all over even if it keeps you here until after the reserve game is over. The power plant must have this part to get steam up for tomorrow."

A feeling something like sitting on the substitute bench during a cold rain and watching the varsity lose the game with Mansfield High—as had happened the season before—was making Andy's knees tremble as he took over the job of finishing the repair part in the lathe.

It seemed the lathe tool was taking *years* to move all but the last eighth of an inch from the small end of the bolt to where the drawing said the cut should stop. Then it seemed the tool would suddenly move faster, and you had to shut off the power feed quickly before you spoiled the job.

Which almost happened as Andy—after he settled down and his knees had quit shaking—was making what he hoped with the final finishing cut. Just then one of the other boys bumped into his elbow and knocked his hand away from the control lever!

He slapped frantically at the control lever, missed, and had to slap it again before the chip stopped curling up from his lathe-tool bit. He was almost afraid to look at the graduations on his machinist's scale when he measured the job—with those cold chills starting his knees to trembling again.

"How are you getting along?" Mr. Stark asked.

Andy, startled by the unexpected question from behind him, almost dropped his steel machinist's scale. "I—I'm afraid I've spoiled it," he said dejectedly.

Mr. Stark was frowning in earnest when he said crossly, "If you have, it's partly my fault. One of the worst blunders a boss can make is to walk up behind a busy man and yell a question at him. The boss should always make sure that the man sees him coming first."

"It wasn't you, sir," said Andy quickly. "Someone else bumped my elbow just as I——"

"That doesn't excuse my blunder," snapped Mr. Stark, then took his own machinist's scale from the little pocket of his shop apron and measured the bolt. "Good enough," he said shortly. "Now scoot for the gym!"

Andy could have hugged Mr. Stark for that. But seniors did not hug anybody—and certainly not Mr. Stark. He took off his shop apron, stuffed it into his tool drawer, and was off for the gymnasium locker room.

Most of the starting line-up of the reserve squad were already on the playing field when Andy ran up to report his presence to Mr. Winthrop. At the far end of the field three complete teams of Mansfield reserves, in green jerseys and faded but clean gold pants, were going through signal drill.

Andy looked them over and said to Mr. Winthrop, "They're bigger than last year."

"Considerably," said Mr. Winthrop, then nodded toward a Mansfield player noticeably shorter than the rest of the boys in his particular eleven. "All but Parks there. But don't let his size fool you. Keep your eye on him; he's the most dangerous player they have. Runs like a scared rabbit and has a good short pass." He nodded toward another man in the same backfield unit. "That's Faulkner. When you see him fading back with the ball, it is always a long pass. Drift back for an interception. But don't leave your middle line backer's position when that stumpy Parks is moving with the ball. He's liable to do anything with it—run straight down the middle or shoot a pass right to the spot you've just left."

Soon after that the officials called the opposing team captains to the center of the field for the coin toss. "Heads for you," said the referee, nodding to Andy, "and tails for you," he added, nodding to Parks, acting as captain for the Mansfield reserves.

He flipped the coin, and it came up tails.

That gave Mansfield the privilege of receiving the kickoff—which Parks promptly chose, leaving Andy the choice of goals to defend. He chose the one which would give him the wind at his back.

The Mansfield players raced to their positions with an aggressiveness that was not overlooked by Andy's teammates. Andy motioned his team into a last-moment huddle and said, "This Mansfield bunch are trying to make us think they are as good as the Mansfield varsity that beat our varsity last season. Let's make 'em prove it!"

A high kick by Andy soared to the ten-yard line. Parks caught it on the dead run. Brown launched a diving tackle at him and missed. Both Riverford tackles had their hands on him, but somehow Parks shook them off and came dodging and side-stepping up the field straight for Andy!

With one hundred and sixty-eight pounds of a perfectly conditioned body behind his shoulder pads as he came charging to meet the ball carrier, Andy suddenly felt that fear he had told his father about the night before—that he might seriously injure this smaller boy.

Then, in just the briefest eyewink before the impact, Andy relaxed the drive in his leg muscles and attempted to catch Parks in his arms . . . Parks burst out of Andy's arms and raced all the way for a touchdown. Then, with a mocking grin on his face, kicked the extra point. The score, after less than thirty seconds of play: Mansfield reserves 7, Riverford reserves 0.

As Andy's teammates dejectedly took up their positions to receive the kickoff, there was only time for him to grab Brown's slack arm and give it a shake. "Forget everybody but Parks. Block him out, and I'll try to make those seven points back on this run."

Andy was running full speed when he caught the ball, with Mansfield's two big tackles converging on him. He lowered his head and split them apart, then straightened up and turned on still more speed . . . He could feel the jar of shoulder pads against his hips and knees as he left a string of prone tacklers behind him.

He was in the clear now except for Parks, who was warily watching Brown out of the corner of his eye as he came in low for his tackle.

Brown tried but missed . . . Andy tried to straight-arm his tackler and shunt him aside, but Parks slipped under his outstretched hand.

Andy felt something almost as bad as the kick of a

mule when stocky little Parks hit his thigh pad with his shoulder. But the tackler's arms did not lock themselves around Andy's knees, and he raced over the goal line.

As he tossed the ball to the field judge, Andy saw Parks get up slowly and walk uncertainly away from his own teammates. Suddenly he whirled around, clapped his hands sharply, and barked, "Come on, let's block this kick!"

Andy took a practice swing with his kicking foot. He backed up one step, keeping his eye on the small bare spot where he had shown his quarterback Jones to place the ball for the try for point after touchdown.

The ball came back. Jones placed it perfectly. Andy knew even before his toe hit the ball that his swing was perfect. Only then did he take his eyes off the spot where the ball had been—looking up confidently for the satisfaction of watching it soar over the crossbar of the goal posts.

Instead he saw a pair of green-clad crossed arms in front of Parks's tense face. His kick had been blocked!

Parks darted over, picked up the loose ball, and handed it to Andy. "That washes up you Riverfords. From now on Mansfield does all the scoring," he said, and walked back to his teammates.

After receiving the next kickoff Mansfield came driving upfield with hard smashes at the two weak spots in the Riverford reserves line—the tackles.

Mansfield was on Riverford's thirty-yard line and driving for another score when Andy walked down the line slapping his guards and tackles sharply on the back. "Submarine—dive under those big tackles and raise up. Block those holes!"

For the next two plays Mansfield's line smashes were stopped. Then, as soon as he saw the defensive tackles were not trying to break through the line, Parks, the Mansfield quarterback, faded back, waited unmolested for his receiver to get downfield, and threw a pass.

Andy was just able to deflect the ball with his finger tips from the waiting hands of its intended receiver.

It was fourth down, with ten yards still to go. Parks dropped back in punt formation. He faked a kick, then streaked for the side lines.

Andy took one step in pursuit, then stopped short. Mr. Winthrop had warned him to stay in his defensive zone whenever Parks was moving with the ball. *But Mr. Winthrop was wrong, dead-wrong, about this play,* Andy was thinking as he watched Brown misjudge Parks's flashing speed and go skidding harmlessly along on his chest behind the ball carrier.

It was too late for Andy to do anything about it. His left line backer was the only man—except little Jones back on the goal line—between Parks and another quick touchdown.

Suddenly Parks cut back to avoid his tackler and darted across the scrimmage line. He couldn't pass now; he would have to run with the ball.

Andy was already off and running as soon as he was sure Parks couldn't possibly cut back again and throw a pass.

Then he hit Parks with a driving tackle that drove him back across the scrimmage line. And at the moment of impact Andy had heard an ominous snap.

Parks lay motionless on his back, eyes closed and a blank expression on his face.

Andy thought his own heart had stopped beating as he dropped to one knee and slid his hands under Parks and started to lift him up in his arms. "Time out!" he yelled. "Parks is hurt—bad!"

Just then Parks's eyes snapped open and he growled at Andy, "Put me down, you big chump. My pants are split clear up the back!"

Andy dropped his burden none too gently and grinned, "If you had been playing on my side, it wouldn't have happened."

Several wide strips of white adhesive tape restored Parks's uniform to at least serviceable playing condition, and play was resumed. But the Mansfield reserves had failed to make a first down and had to give up possession of the ball on Riverford's twenty-five-yard line.

Jones, quarterback for the Riverford reserves and the lightest boy on the field by ten pounds, sent Andy over left guard for twelve yards. He almost broke into the clear, but Parks came racing up from his deep safety position and cut Andy's feet from under him with a low tackle.

Parks bounced to his feet and said tauntingly, "I've found out how to cut you down to my size, you big ox," and trotted back to his defense position.

Three times more Andy ripped through the now confused and disorganized Mansfield line. And each time it was Parks who made the tackle.

The referee placed the ball down on the fifty-yard line and signaled to the head linesman that Riverford had made another first down.

Back in the huddle Jones hitched up his hip pads and said, "We've got Parks running up on every play to stop

Andy. This time Brown goes down and cuts in. Andy, you heave one of those long ones on the dead run, the way you did in practice. Let's go!"

Andy took a direct pass from center and ran toward the right sideline, with only little Jones running ahead of him as interference. He kept angling back a little toward his own goal line in an effort to decoy the Mansfield right end into position for a block by Jones.

As though he were trying to run right through his larger opponent, Jones put all the power of his one hundred and twenty pounds behind his left shoulder pad as he dove into the end.

Then, with what looked like an open field between him and the goal line—except for Parks, who was running up, Andy jammed his cleats into the turf and broke back for mid-field again.

Far down there on the twenty-yard line stood Brown waiting, almost pleading, for the ball—and flapping his hands as if his wrists were broken. Andy whipped the ball to him without breaking, then raced back in the direction from which he had just come to protect the most vulnerable spot on the field against a pass interception and a dazzling runback by Parks.

But all Parks could do was whirl around in frantic pursuit of Brown, who by then was racing over the goal line with the ball tightly clutched in his arms. Andy made the extra point this time with a perfect kick.

After that the Mansfield reserves seemed to fall apart —except Parks, who grew more aggressive with every play.

But what turned the first half into almost a rout was little Jones's faking the ball to Andy and then following his fullback through the line. Andy brushed Parks aside with a shoulder block, and Jones went untouched for sixty yards and another score.

As the team trotted off the field at half-time intermission, the score stood Riverford reserves 27, Mansfield reserves 7.

Mr. Winthrop moved among his boys, checking up on possible injuries that they might be concealing to keep from missing a chance to play in the second half. Then, apparently satisfied with their condition, he turned to the boys who had sat on the substitute bench during the first half and said, "All of you start warming up. Keep moving!"

Three minutes before the second half was to begin, the Mansfield reserves came racing back into the field, clapping their hands and shouting words of encouragement to each other.

Mr. Winthrop motioned the entire Riverford squad to gather around him. "I'm starting ten new men this half," he announced, then named them . . . "Jones stays in."

"You mean Carter, don't you, Mr. Winthrop?" said Shorty, pointing to Andy.

With a mild twinkle in his eye Mr. Winthrop looked at Jones and said, "Jones or Carter—whichever one expects to be a varsity quarterback next season."

"That's me, then," said Shorty sheepishly.

Mr. Winthrop turned to the ten new boys who were to start the second half and jerked his thumb over his shoulder at the Mansfield team. "Those fellows are out for revenge. They'll take it out on you if you let 'em. But if you let 'em cross our goal line—out the whole tribe of you come . . . You, Jones—anybody who talks back in the huddle or fails to carry out his assignment, send him to the side lines!"

With his hand on Andy's arm Mr. Winthrop walked back to the side-line bench and sat down. He rested his hands, relaxed, on his knees and said, "Now let's see how much they absorbed from the running lecture I gave them while you boys were out there."

For the first few minutes of the second half the aggressiveness of the Mansfield team made Andy uneasy. Faulkner began smashing through the line just as he had at the beginning of the game.

Then the Riverford guards started submarining, stopping those fullback plunges at the scrimmage line.

"Parks will send Faulkner back for that long pass," said Mr. Winthrop to Andy. "Now we'll see if Phillips remembers what you did to cover it."

Faulkner dropped back to pass. Phillips, out there in Andy's former position as middle line backer, turned and ran back ten yards. He stood stock-still while the ball smacked into his hands as though it had been intended for him originally.

Mr. Winthrop relaxed his momentary tenseness and chuckled. "Parks is too smart to call that play again . . . But he isn't through yet. Just wait, that boy won't quit trying to win this game right up to the last play."

Almost before Mr. Winthrop had finished speaking, Parks sent his fullback Faulkner back as safety man and moved up into the middle line backer spot himself. Immediately his unerring tackles slowed down the line plunges of the Riverford backs. Singlehanded he brought their goalward drive to a halt.

Jones sent Phillips back to punt on fourth down. It was not a very good punt, but the ball took a crazy bounce as Faulkner was reaching for it. Brown, Riverford's right end, hit him with a crashing tackle. Coming out of nowhere, Jones dove on the ball, with Parks right on top of him clawing frantically to steal the ball.

On the very next play Jones, on a quarterback sneak play, skipped over for a touchdown.

Without any preliminary explanation Mr. Winthrop said over his shoulder to Andy, "Keep your eye on Parks. You're going to see him in action again when the Mansfield varsity plays our varsity in November or I don't know top-grade football material when I see it."

But the Mansfield reserves had lost their aggressiveness. They played listlessly through the third quarter and grew steadily less effective as the fourth quarter drew to a close.

All of them but Parks—who continued to tackle and block as though his team held a one-point advantage and he was racing against the clock to protect it.

"It's all over now," said Andy, leaning forward to rush out onto the field to congratulate his teammates.

Mr. Winthrop placed his hand on Andy's arm. "Wait, Parks has time for one more play."

Andy was not looking in that direction when Parks suddenly burst through at his own fifteen-yard line and raced the length of the field for a touchdown. With cool assurance he kicked the extra point, and the game was over . . . Riverford reserves 33, Mansfield reserves 14.

While the ball was still bouncing around behind the goal posts, Parks whirled and ran over to meet Andy, who was running onto the field to congratulate his team-mates.

Parks tossed Andy a half-admiring, half-taunting grin and said, "It's a good thing for you, you big ox, that you are a senior. Because next year I'll be almost as big as you, and I would run all over you!"

"How do you like that?" said Phillips, who had been standing close by. "He wasn't sport enough to offer to shake hands."

But Andy didn't mind. He had been paid the finest compliment a football player can receive—by the best man on the field, and a rival at that.

Back in the locker room after the game Andy was about to remove his jersey when Coach Dorman opened the door of his office and called out, "Carter!" and closed the door again.

Andy clattered the length of the locker room in his football shoes to obey the summons.

"Close the door behind you, Carter," said Coach Dorman curtly. He paused to look intently at Andy. "It seems that I have to break a lifelong rule of mine every time I talk to you. This time I am offering you a *second* chance to move up to the varsity squad."

Andy was trying to think of what to say when Coach Dorman checked him with an upraised hand. "Let me finish first. The varsity is going to need a good place-kicking and kickoff specialist to help win the close games this season. Mr. Winthrop reports that you did well at this in the reserve game this afternoon."

The coach settled himself more comfortably in his chair and resumed. "Understand, I am *not* promising you a varsity letter. In fact, I am asking you to decide on the basis *that you haven't an outside chance to* get one. Now what's your answer?"

Andy looked down at the floor, thinking to himself, *Since you've got to play football only for fun, stay with the reserves, where everybody looks up to you.*

"Take your time, Carter," said Coach Dorman in a sudden change of tone. "I know it is a tough question to answer, and it has to be answered once and for all. I won't ask you again."

Slowly Andy raised his eyes and said, "Varsity."

Coach Dorman nodded. "Report for practice with the varsity Monday, then. Use any third-stringers loafing around to center and chase balls for you. And try to teach at least two boys to hold the ball for you when place-kicking. That's all, Carter."

Chapter 11

A cold drizzling rain had been falling most of the night when Andy came down to breakfast. His father was reading the morning paper, waiting for the coffee in the electric percolator on the table to finish brewing.

He glanced up at Andy and said, "Too bad; it looks as if the rain is going to spoil the game with Grant this afternoon for Susie and her friends."

"It will stop before noon and clear up," said Andy, performing his regular morning duty by plugging in the automatic toaster and getting the first batch of toast started.

"Paper doesn't agree with you," said his father, glancing again at the weather prediction for the day.

"Oh, that was turned in around midnight," said Andy. "My information is later. I just heard a radio ham over in Illinois say the rain had moved east and it was clearing up over there. That's only about a hundred miles from here, so it should be clear by the time the game starts, at two-thirty."

His father looked over the top of his paper and said, "The more I see of the way amateur radio enthusiasts can pick information like that out of thin air the more I think, Son, that *electronics* is the thing you should specialize in when you go to college. Why, you don't have to pay any rent for the use of the air to send messages—music—pictures—advertising." He paused to smile, adding, "Now if you'll just invent a way of selling fire insurance to people without having to keep calling back time after time, you've made a million dollars right now."

Just then Susie came downstairs—at least five minutes earlier than usual. Andy gave the clock a look of astonishment and clutched dramatically at his heart but said nothing.

"I just want to see what the paper says about the reserve game yesterday," she announced.

"I know; you want the comic section," said her father, and handed it over.

Susie, however, ignored her favorite newspaper feature, the comic page, and began scanning the sports page, which faced it.

After reading a brief item tucked away under a bowling league score she gave a little bounce of indignation and said, "I'll bet anything the sports editor of this paper graduated from Mansfield High!"

"He went to high school in Chicago," Andy informed her. "I know, because he told us he did at the football banquet last season."

"Then somebody is paying him to *belittle* Riverford," said Susie indignantly. "All he says here about the wonderful way we positively *murdered* those Mansfield reserves yesterday afternoon is just the score, and that their boy Parks was the outstanding player on the field."

"He was," said Andy, speaking with the conviction of an eyewitness.

"How many touchdowns did *he* make?" inquired Susie, cross-examining her brother.

"Two, and kicked both points afterward," said Andy.

"And, pray, Mr. Carter, how many did my own brother, on the Riverford team, make—*pray?*"

"Two, I think," admitted Andy, "but I had a lot more help for mine."

"That's just why I think the paper is unfair," said Susie vehemently. "You only played *half* the game, and you were so good that Mr. Winthrop felt sorry for Mansfield and kept you out of the second half. But it took this Parks boy a whole game to make his two. And now they say he was the, quote, 'outstanding player on the field,' unquote."

"Who is ready for toast?" inquired Andy.

His father put aside his paper and nodded to Andy. "That's right; when your facts bounce off, a change of subject is your only defense against a woman's arguments."

"What is this about a woman's argument?" smilingly inquired Mrs. Carter, bringing a piping-hot platter of bacon and eggs from the kitchen.

With a charitable sigh that had a touch of pity in it, Susie said, "Papa was just admitting that men aren't bright enough to win an argument with us women."

Mrs. Carter arched an eyebrow at her husband and poured his coffee. But she said nothing.

That afternoon Andy found himself dressed in his school clothes—just another student spectator at a football game. He was sitting high up in the stands, where he had sat as a freshman.

Down front he could see Susie, seated almost in the strategic center of a block of girls who were all wearing the official insignia of Riverford's intensely loyal Sophomorettes, a large rosette of blue and gold crepe paper with long streamers. It would have been hard for Andy to miss noticing Susie, because she kept jumping up and waving to her late-coming friends—which meant just about everyone from Riverford High.

Down on the playing field the Riverford players were going through their pregame warm-up—short sprints—passing the ball to one another—and taking practice dives and roll-overs on the damp, yielding turf. Ken Blair made several short zigzagging runs to test how well his cleats were holding, then began tossing easy passes to Cornstalk and the other ends.

Once Cornstalk stopped and looked up into the stands. Andy could almost feel his friend's eyes looking into his. But Cornstalk turned and trotted upfield without smiling or waving.

Andy had smiled at Cornstalk, but he understood why he had not received a smile in return. He remembered how all those faces had looked to him when he was down there just before the start of the game. You were trying to pretend that you were just taking things easy, but inside all you were thinking about was—well, you couldn't have recognized your own father up in the stands unless he stood up and waved a red umbrella at you.

It was almost time for the kickoff now. The Grant High team was gathered around their coach, their helmets under their arms. Two tall but rather slim boys with blond hair were standing with their backs to Andy. These he recognized without difficulty as the twin ends Mr. Dorman had talked about. And, of course, he could recognize Wilson, their fullback, who stood a half head taller than the rest. Andy had played against Wilson in a reserve game when they both were sophomores; he remembered how his head buzzed after tackling him the first time—yes, and how he flinched every time after that.

Andy stopped thinking about the past, because Eddins had just kicked off and the ball was soaring high in the air. The strong wind seemed to stop it in mid-flight. It came almost straight down on the twenty-five-yard line and took an erratic bounce, back toward mid-field.

One of Grant's twin-brother ends snatched it grace-fully out of the air and darted across the field where his brother was waiting to block for him. Ken Blair came running up and clamped his arms around the knees of one of the twins, downing him with a clean tackle. A man sitting next to Andy jumped up and yelled, "That's the way to do it, Son!"

Andy, who had kept his eyes on the ball itself, in-stinctively saw the tackled twin flip a backward pass to his brother—who went streaking on down the side-lines with it for a touchdown.

"Foul! Foul! Call that play back!" the man next to Andy was yelling. "That first boy was down before he passed that ball."

Apparently all three officials on the field had a dif-ferent opinion, because the touchdown was allowed. Then with one twin holding the other kicked the extra point. Andy could not tell which one, but he was ready to bet that it was the one who didn't carry the ball over the goal line. Then he glanced sidelong at the red-faced man sitting next to him. It was Ken Blair's father.

Riverford failed to recover from this stunning sur-prise until well into the second quarter. Ken was trying harder than any other player on the field—a bit too hard—and was pressing, Andy suspected. But somehow his flashing end runs were stopped at the scrimmage line by one or the other of Grant's twin-brother ends. And when he dropped back to pass, the twins crashed in and hurried his passing.

"My boy is the only Riverford player even *trying*," burst out Ken's father indignantly. "He's getting no protection for his passes. Look at the way they let those two Grant ends rush him."

It was third down just then, and Andy said over his shoulder, "They'll do that once too often to Ken. Watch for him to throw one to the flat, to that tall right end."

Which is exactly what Ken did on the very next play. Having decoyed both Grant ends in, he flipped a sharp pass out to Cornstalk. And when Cornstalk had a football in his big hands and a one-stride handicap on a line backer, only a man as fast as Parks of the Mansfield reserves could catch him.

Cornstalk finished his triumphant gallop with a one-handed cartwheel in the end zone. After which he decorously flipped the ball to the referee.

Coach Dorman sent in Beck, who did nothing but kick points after touchdowns. Beck made a perfect kick and returned to the substitute bench. Andy found himself wondering if he would ever be as cool under pressure as Beck.

There was no more scoring until after the start of the fourth quarter. One of Grant's twin-brother ends dropped back, instead of rushing in on Ken's pass play, and intercepted the ball to run for Grant's second score. The other twin was not in the game at the time. It was

Wilson, the Grant fullback, who attempted the kick. But Walker of Riverford broke through to block it.

The scoreboard clock—built, incidentally, by Mr. Stark in his spare time—indicated there was only two minutes to go. Ken's father looked at it and said, "Ken will never make it up now. There just isn't time!"

Andy was thinking the same thing, but for a reason that he didn't think Ken's father would like to hear. It was because Ken had been trying all during the game to make touchdowns himself and had only called on his other backs, including Eddins, for short gains to make a yard or two for a first down.

Apparently Coach Dorman was of the same opinion; for just as the Riverford team was lining up to receive the kickoff, he sent in Marshall, a sophomore quarterback, to replace Ken.

"What on earth is that coach thinking about?" demanded Ken's father indignantly. "My boy is the only one who can gain big yardage."

"Maybe," suggested Andy diplomatically, "Marshall is coming in with a quick scoring play." Actually he did not expect any such thing. He knew that Eddins and the other backs were perfectly capable of driving the full length of the field if they put their hearts into it—something, it was plain, they had not been doing up until then.

Marshall caught the kickoff. Eddins gave him a block that took out one of the twin-brother ends. Cornstalk took care of the other end. Big, hard-charging Walker bumped one Grant player to the ground, then thundered downfield for Grant's safety man.

Marshall was tackled by Wilson, Grant's fullback, on the mid-field stripe.

Ken's father nudged Andy with his elbow. "What is this trick play they will pull next?"

"You've just seen it," said Andy vaguely, but without taking his eyes off Marshall, who was crouched behind his center. Marshall fed the ball to Eddins, who burst through a hole torn in the Grant line by a ferocious charge by Walker . . . Then Cornstalk threw a block . . . There were blocks being thrown all over the field.

Eddins—not a particularly fast runner—lurched and stumbled to the ten-yard line.

"You mean, *there* was the trick play!" Ken's father chuckled. "I'll take back what I said about your coach, boy. That fellow is *tricky*."

Andy didn't think it was his business to explain that it was only a straight piece of football—a line buck which had gained all those yards because every Riverford player had carried out his assignment.

Marshall used up three downs and gained just four yards. Then suddenly Ken raced back onto the field with his arm uplifted. He relieved Marshall, and the referee paced off a five-yard penalty against Riverford.

"The robber!" exclaimed Ken's father explosively.

"It's a five-yard penalty for delaying play," explained Andy, beginning to doubt Coach Dorman's judgment himself.

His doubts increased when he thought he saw Ken take the ball, bury it in the pit of his stomach, and race around end—where one of the twins was crouched waiting for him.

Then, to his astonishment, he saw the striped sleeves

of the field judge upraised. Eddins had smashed over Walker's position for another touchdown! Beck trotted in and kicked the extra point.

Andy was almost knocked off his feet as Ken's father started down for the playing field to his hero son. Andy looked at the scoreboard: Riverford 14, Visitors 13.

From high up in his old seat Andy watched Susie and her Sophomorettes tear their crepe-paper colors into confetti and toss it into the air as they joined in the school victory yell.

Of course he had no way of knowing it, but up in the tiny press box the sports reporter for the morning paper was tapping out a new first paragraph for his story: "Showing just two minutes of real teamwork, Riverford marched the length of the field in the closing moments of the game to win from Grant High by the slimmest of margins, one point that was delivered by the precision toe of Tommy Beck. . . . Overshadowing the play of all the others on both teams was the performance of Grant's twin-brother ends, Ralph and Fred Dyer . . ."

Chapter 12

There was a hint of autumn crispness in the air when Andy arrived at the football practice field the Monday afternoon following that close game with Grant High.

Coach Dorman was busy having the first- and second-string varsity teams walk through a new play they were to use the coming Friday in the game with Trenton. Andy, following the instruction Coach Dorman had given him the previous Thursday afternoon, went on down to the practice field goal posts and began his place-kicking practice.

A little later Coach Dorman sent the varsity linemen to the blocking and tackling dummies. Mr. Ellerly came down to where Andy was practicing and, after watching him critically for a few place kicks, said, "You are putting down your left foot a little too close to the ball, Carter. Remember your geometry: your right leg should swing parallel to your left, and your right toe should strike the center of the ball—not to one side as you are doing it."

Andy tried it that way and made a perfect field goal.

"That's about all there is to it," said Mr. Ellery, and walked back upfield.

As soon as Mr. Ellerly was out of earshot, Walker, the big senior tackle, came over to Andy and said, "Hey, did you see the newspaper clipping about the Grant game that we stuck with adhesive tape on Ken's locker?"

"I did," said Andy, and kicked another perfect goal. "But I don't think it was good tactics."

"Ken has it coming to him," said Walker disgustedly.

Andy turned and looked Walker over, from his close-cropped crew cut down over his brawny shoulders to his feet, then back up to his eyes. "Look, Walker, if you're trying to hint to Ken what I think you are, the best way to do it is for you seniors to take him aside and give it to him, man to man."

Walker said, "That's what I wanted to do. But Cornstalk says he won't poke his nose into it. And Eddins says it would look as if he were jealous of Ken." He paused and grinned frankly at Andy. "You know me. If I walked up and told him and he got fresh about it, I'd slap him one. Anybody who doesn't play team play without being told, I've got no use for."

Walker turned to go back to tackling and blocking drill, but suddenly retraced his steps and gave Andy a meaningful squint. "I just thought of something. You're a senior, too. You're the one to get Ken back on the right track with the rest of the team. He can't get sore at you because you're just a—well, I mean you don't run around yapping at people; so when you do, they listen."

Without committing himself on the subject of Ken, Andy looked Walker straight in the eye and said, "Maybe I'd better start practicing on you."

"O.K., let's have it," said Walker, grinning. "But if you're going to tell me I wasn't opening holes in that Grant line the way I should, I already know that. I didn't get going until that big two-hundred-pounder came in for Meyers."

"You didn't have any trouble moving Meyers last year," Andy reminded him.

Walker wagged his head, baffled. "That's what kept

worrying me all the time Meyers was in there. Last year I could move him as if he were stuffed with feathers. But this year he either blocked me cold or slipped past me and played tag with our backfield—grab-and-hold tag, at that."

"I can tell you why," said Andy, resting his hands on his hips, then freeing his right to point at Walker's big feet. "Meyers learned last year to read your feet. You tip off your opponent every time which way you are going to charge."

"O.K.," said Walker, assuming his offensive line position. "Let's see you get past me to make a tackle. And to make it tougher, you can say 'Go' for the ball-snap."

Without stopping to think that neither one of them was wearing a helmet, Andy accepted the challenge. At his bark of "Go!" he bunted Walker aside with his hands and slipped past him.

"Try it again," demanded Walker. Then, after failing to block Andy even once in six attempts, Walker suddenly straightened up and said, "I holler 'Uncle.' What do I do with my feet that gives me away?"

Andy rubbed a lump on his eyebrow that was swelling rapidly from a collision with Walker's head and said, "Your feet are as easy to read as that newspaper clipping. When you are going to charge to the left you pull your left foot back about an inch. When you charge to your right, the right one shifts back. And on a straight-ahead charge you don't shift either."

"Thanks," said Walker grimly. "Anybody else who does what Meyers did to me in the Grant game will have to be a mind reader."

Just then Coach Dorman walked up. He took one

look at a drop of blood oozing from the lump on Andy's eyebrow and said curtly, "How many times do I have to say it? You boys are not to engage in man-to-man contact without helmets."

He pulled a bottle from his hip pocket and swabbed Andy's eyebrow with antiseptic. "Now keep your dirty hands away from that cut. And if the bleeding doesn't stop right away, take a shower and go to Dr. Clark's office and have him patch you up."

Walker watched Andy receiving first aid, then—as soon as Coach Dorman was out of hearing—he gave Andy a remindful poke in the ribs. "Remember, it's your job to make a team player out of Ken Blair. We don't care how you do it. But we plan to take that last game against Mansfield if we have to throw Ken off the field and play with just ten men to do it!"

Andy watched the big tackle go back to the tackling dummy and slam into it with his shoulder. If any other member of the squad had talked like that, Andy would have dismissed it from his mind as what he called "wild talk" then and there. Coming from Walker, it worried him.

Again, in the locker room after practice, Andy saw more evidence of the seriousness of the feud between the seniors and their junior quarterback. Walker was picking over the pile of shower bath towels, looking, as usual, for an extra-big one, when Ken Blair called over to him, "Throw me one, too."

Walker took his time until he found a ragged one about two thirds of its original size. He flung it to Ken.

Andy thought Ken was going to get fighting-mad for a minute. He had torn the clipping off his locker door without comment, but it was obvious that he was simmering. He just threw the towel hard on the floor, went to the pile and picked out a better one. Then he tossed another towel to Andy, saying, "This is for that running-pass stunt you showed me. It was the only one that worked during the game today."

Andy was too surprised to say more than "Thanks" before Ken had disappeared into the shower room.

All during practice that week Andy kept wondering why the coaches, Mr. Dorman and Mr. Ellerly, couldn't see that the feud was growing worse and do something about it. But Coach Dorman only seemed to make matters worse by commenting several times on the poor blocking and line play of the team in the Grant game, and warning that their next game would be against a more aggressive and better drilled team, Trenton High.

The feud almost broke out into the open on Thursday, the day before the Trenton game, when Walker said, "You're right, Coach. They haven't any star; you've got to watch all eleven of them all the time."

Coach Dorman gave Walker a level look and said bitingly, "When eleven men all perform their assignments perfectly, you have a team of *eleven* stars."

But it was plain to Andy soon after the game with Trenton started that the feud was still smoldering out there on the playing field. This time, however, the seniors had changed their "treatment." The first time Riverford got the ball on a punt from Trenton, the linemen charged with precision, and Ken's backfield blockers ruthlessly mowed down his would-be tacklers.

Except for three third-down line plunges by Eddins,

Ken carried the ball, on end runs and cutbacks through tackle, to the five-yard line.

At this point Andy began to hope that Ken would have the good sense to send Eddins over for the score. Instead Ken flashed through a gaping hole, opened up by Walker's crashing charge, and scored. Beck came in, kicked the extra point, and returned to the substitute bench.

That was the only score made by either team during the first half. The Trenton team seemed to have solved Ken's deceptive running style. When he tried his long running pass that Andy had taught him, Cornstalk was down there waiting for it—only to have a Trenton lineman break through and throw the passer for a five-yard loss.

During the half-time rest period Coach Dorman faced his varsity squad with a worried look. "You are doing fine on defense," he told them. "Trenton has gained only twenty yards by rushing; and their passing game has been bottled up nicely—thanks principally to two pass interceptions by Blair, one by Eddins, and the way Walker has been breaking through their line."

Coach Dorman reached down and pulled a blade of grass, then tossed it aside, shaking his head. "But outside of that first drive your offensive play has been ragged. You've been missing first downs by less than a yard—almost inches sometimes. Now let's hitch up our pants and go for that extra inch and yard in the second half!" He turned and walked out to mid-field for a brief social visit with the game officials, leaving the squad to relax before the starting whistle of the second half.

Andy shoved Walker over to make room for himself

on the grass between the big varsity tackle and Corn-stalk, who was lying on his stomach with his chin propped in his hands, chewing unconcernedly on a blade of grass.

"Keep your big hands off my shoulders," growled Walker, more than half in earnest. "They're both sore."

"I wish I had a club, the way you fellows have blown up," Andy retorted.

"I'm doing pretty well, if anybody wants to know," said Walker, unruffled. "I've already worn out two Trenton guys trying to stop me." He jerked his head sideward in Cornstalk's direction, on Andy's other side, adding, "Nobody has turned Cornstalk's end yet. And it isn't his fault that the ball didn't get down to him those three times he was behind their safety man."

Since he could not deny those facts Andy tried another approach. "Now look, fellows, this is the first chance any of us has had to play on a championship team. We can't go on winning games by one point or by only one touchdown. We've got to, as my dad says, protect ourselves with *insurance* against the unexpected. Touchdowns, I mean, and as many as we can get. If we don't, one of these days we'll hear the closing gun of the game on the short end of the score. And there goes our championship!"

Cornstalk kept on chewing his grass stem—looking straight ahead but saying nothing.

Walker gave Andy an accusing side glance. "You aren't holding up your end so well, either, I notice. We're still having to take the same old thing." He nodded over to where Ken Blair was tossing up a handful of grass to test whether there had been any change in wind direction, adding in a grim undertone, "When you hang a lamp shade over that bright and shining light, you will be able to see ten other stars start shining."

The game officials started walking to their positions. The squad got leisurely to their feet. As Andy turned to resume his seat on the substitute bench, Walker bumped him with his shoulder and said, "Don't worry; if Trenton scores, we'll come right back with two more. We're not *that* sore at anybody, to blow a chance for the championship. *Ken* isn't worth it!"

Right from the first whistle of the second half Andy's fellow seniors demonstrated by their playing that they intended to give him the "insurance," in the way of at least another quick touchdown, he had asked for. No matter who was carrying the ball, Walker ripped big holes in the Trenton line. And the two halfbacks blocked just as hard for Ken as they did for Eddins or for each other.

But with the beginning of the fourth quarter Andy could see why Coach Dorman was pacing up and down the side lines. It was because Ken Blair, as quarterback, had lost his usually keen sense of timing. Twice he had failed to pull his left foot out of the way when feeding the ball to Eddins, causing Eddins to trip and fall at the line of scrimmage.

Ken seemed to grow tenser as the game moved into the fourth quarter. On third down, with less than a yard to go—which Eddins could have made easily through a hole that Walker opened up—Ken fumbled the ball for the first time that Andy could remember!

Andy held his breath while the referee untangled the pile of players covering the fumbled ball. Then he saw the last man to be pulled off—Ken, with the ball clutched so tightly that the official had to pry his hands from it.

Ken dropped back to his own twenty-five-yard line to punt on fourth down—and fumbled the ball again!

A hollow groan went up from the Riverford cheering section as the referee signaled to the head lineman that Trenton had recovered on Riverford's fifteen-yard line.

The Trenton team came racing out of the huddle, eager for a touchdown. But three times the Riverford line stopped the ball carrier in his tracks.

Andy was off the bench now, crouched forward with his fists clenched in suspense. He knew what was on the next play: the Trenton quarterback would snap a quick pass out to his big right end, who had been threatening all afternoon to score.

Andy's prediction was wrong—that right end was coming around for the old Statue-of-Liberty play. And the whole Riverford secondary had been pulled out of defensive position by a fake fullback smash into the right side of the Trenton line. Even Ken had raced forward to stop it.

Suddenly the Trenton end stopped short and cocked his arm while he coolly waited for his own left end to cut back through the end zone to the right-hand corner.

Andy dropped his chin and covered his eyes with his hands. At least he didn't have to look at it——

An explosive roar from the Riverford rooting section went up. Andy spread his fingers just a little—then jumped to his feet as though to keep his heart from popping out of his mouth . . . Walker was just getting up, wearing a smug but grim smile, after tackling the passer

—still with the ball in his hand—back on the twenty-five-yard line.

Ken was walking groggily in a circle. Eddins had to catch him by both shoulders and turn him around. Ken leaned over, shook his head rapidly, then suddenly straightened up and clapped his hands sharply.

Up at the other end of the substitute bench Coach Dorman was waving his arms to attract somebody's attention out on the field and making kicking motions with his right foot.

Walker gave Ken's arm a hard shake and pointed toward Coach Dorman. Ken nodded and was dropping back in punt formation when the referee picked up the ball and paced off a five-yard penalty against Riverford for too much time in the huddle.

Ken managed to get his punt away. It was not one of his best punts, rolling out of bounds on Riverford's forty-yard line.

Once more in possession of the ball, Trenton lined up in passing formation. But this time the quarterback moved out to right end, and the tall Trenton right end was openly advertising what he proposed doing—even to pulling up his right sleeve and licking his finger tips with his tongue.

He did not get that pass away. Walker again crashed in and tackled him. Undismayed, the big Trenton end went through the same routine—and again Walker tackled him.

Then, *for the third time,* standing on the fifty-yard line, the tall Trenton end went through his prepassing routine—this time drawing a jeering laugh from the Riverford cheering section. With only barely enough time left for one more play, Andy relaxed. But only for a split second. Suddenly he recognized that big Trenton end: *It was Townsend, the president of the dramatic club at Trenton—an accomplished actor.*

"Cornstalk!" yelled Andy, calling the first name that entered his head. "Get back, get back!"

Again big, confident Walker came charging through the Trenton line—unmolested this time. But just as he was about to drive his shoulder into the passer, Trenton's quarterback cut him down with a rolling block.

The ball soared high over Marshall's head into the waiting hands of Trenton's left end. He whirled as he caught it and streaked for Riverford's goal line.

The groan of dismay rising from the Riverford cheering section and the jubilant cheer from across the field from Trenton rooters ended in a clap of silence. For—seemingly out of nowhere—came a flash of blue and gold that cut the Trenton end's feet from under him on the one-yard line.

The official timer's pistol cracked flatly. Cornstalk languidly rose to his feet and looked toward Andy, standing motionless at the farther end of the substitute bench.

Cornstalk clasped his hands over his head in a double sign of triumph and gratitude and broke into a broad grin for Andy. Then he pointed to the scoreboard: *Riverford 7, Visitors 0.*

Chapter 13

That evening as the Carters enjoyed an hour of relaxation in the living room after dinner, Susie slumped in her favorite armchair, staring glumly into space. After about ten minutes of this pointed silence Mr. Carter laid down his newspaper and said to Andy with a subdued twinkle in his eye, "Didn't you say that Riverford won the game with Trenton this afternoon?"

Andy looked up from his radio magazine.

"*Ah,* yes," Susie sighed, "but a hollow victory—empty as a deserted tomb half buried in the desert sands."

"A little too close for comfort, but we won just the same," said Andy.

Susie gave a sudden bounce of outraged sympathy and said, *"You're* the one who should be eating his heart out, not me."

Andy closed the magazine a little reluctantly. "I'm no more to blame for that low score than you are. I was just a bench warmer."

"Oh, *Andy,*" said his mother sympathetically, "didn't you play even *one* quarter?"

"Not one single minute, not one single play!" exclaimed Susie indignantly. "And you can't realize, Mother, how I was *humiliated.* When the clouds of defeat looked darkest, I told the other loyal Sophomorettes not to worry, that Coach Dorman was only waiting for the *dramatic* moment to call on Andy to save the day. We kept chanting, 'We want Andy! We want Andy!' But Coach Dorman, who was right down there in front of us, simply wouldn't pay any attention."

"After all," suggested Mr. Carter, "the team won. And Andy is a member of that team. Even if he sat out the game on the bench he did his assigned part with the rest."

"I do feel," said their mother, coming to Susie's rescue, "that it was not exactly fair to Andy. He has practiced faithfully and he has been setting a good example for the others by studying hard. I should think the coach could have let him play at least a few minutes. After all, this is Andy's last year. Surely sentiment has its place even in football."

"Not in a close game, it hasn't," said Andy, smiling at his mother. "It's strictly business with the coach. He's paid to win football games, not to lose them like a little gentleman."

It was his father's turn to shake his head. But he was not smiling when he said to Andy, "In some few big colleges, yes. Not in high schools, Son."

Andy felt his ears growing warm under his father's quiet rebuke.

Mrs. Carter glanced sidelong at her husband and said, with a quick little smile for him, "At least you've got to admit the boys have some grounds for thinking the way they do. You know very well that there were certain influential businessmen in Riverford who were unhappy because Mr. Skiles, the last coach, wasn't what they called a 'winning coach.' "

Mr. Carter quickly changed the subject by asking, "Who is going to a movie show with Mother and me?"

Andy shook his head. "Thanks just the same; I'm

working in the basement tonight on the steel rack for my radio transmitter."

Susie looked forlornly at her mother and said, *"Why did I promise Mrs. Doctor Arnold to sit with their baby tonight?"*

"Because," her mother reminded her, "you are earning money for the material for the formal I promised to make—for the *Goblins* party. Remember?"

Susie laid a finger alongside her nose and said, "That r-e-m-i-n-d-s me. I haven't given Rocky Jenkins a chance to ask me to go yet!"

"Supposing he doesn't ask?" inquired Andy.

"He will after the disciplinary committee of the Sophomorettes gets through with him," Susie said. "Willie Brice tried that on Arline Mainerd, our Exalted Scribe. He nearly died of *fright.*"

None of the family asked how Willie Brice had been brought to see the error of his ways. Which Susie took for granted was really a silence of breathless suspense. So, after making sure everyone was paying attention, she added, "We didn't actually threaten him exactly. All we did was promise to bring his baby picture to school and show it to everyone."

"As I recall it," said her father, blundering headlong into the trap, "Willie was quite a handsome baby. I remember how his father used to show us his picture at the slightest opportunity."

Mrs. Carter wrinkled her nose impishly and said, "Have you forgotten, Will, how you used to carry Andy's baby picture in your wallet?"

"But that was different," said Susie. "Andy had his picture taken *with his clothes on.*"

141

Mr. Carter was suddenly seized with a severe coughing spell and had to cover his face with his handkerchief. Mrs. Carter rushed to the kitchen for the cherry-flavored cough syrup. Andy picked up his magazine and went down to his workshop in the basement.

It was after eight o'clock before Andy paused in his laborious task of making a bolt hole in the piece of iron with a small hand drill. He could hear footsteps passing through the house.

Automatically he called out, "Hey, go back and close the front door!"

The footsteps retraced their path, then returned, and eventually Ted Hall clumped down the basement stairs. "You must be a mind reader or something," he said, peering at Andy through his thick eyeglasses. "How did you know I left your front door open?"

"Because somebody always has to close it after you, and there was no one else to do it this time," said Andy.

Ted regarded him intently for a moment, then said, "Maybe you do have *penetrating perception* after all."

"Like what?" said Andy, preparing to resume his labors with a very dull drill and making a mental note to take it to school Monday and have Mr. Stark show him how to sharpen it properly.

"It probably means understanding why people act the way they do," said Ted. "For instance—well, all the trouble Ken Blair has got himself into with you varsity seniors."

"I'm not mixed up in any trouble with Ken," said Andy firmly.

"I guess that's why Ken's father says you have penetrating perception," said Ted as though that explained everything.

Andy replaced the dull drill with a smaller one that looked a little sharper. "You can't start in the middle with a story and expect people to find out for themselves what you're driving at. When did Ken's father get mixed up in this?"

"And how I wish he hadn't!" Ted sighed. "You've got no idea, man, the troubles that are dumped on a student manager of a football team. I'll bet if I got paid only fifty cents an hour for just the time I worry about things I'd be making more money than Coach Dorman."

Andy picked up Ted's left wrist, looked at his friend's strap watch, and said, "At nine o'clock I'm going upstairs and tune in on the forty-meter ham band. So you'd better get down to cases."

Ted gave the watch a startled look and said, "I've got to get going! My father said to hurry back with the car! This is his regular lodge night, and election of officers to boot!"

Ted was gone and out the front door before Andy could ask him more about Ken's father. He sighed with disgust, turned out the light over his workbench, and went up to close the front door, which was standing wide open and letting in a lot of cold air, as usual.

Shortly after ten o'clock he heard his father and mother come home from the movie. There was so much crackling and buzzing mixed up with the weak code signals he was trying to read with his short-wave receiver that he snapped off the switch and hung up his headphones.

Just then his father came in and dropped a paper box

143

of buttered popcorn on the table, saying, "How was the listening tonight?"

"Poor," said Andy, shaking out a mound of popcorn into his palm. "Sounded just like the time last winter when the northern lights were all over half the sky, but maybe not quite that bad."

"Your mother was right, as usual," said Mr. Carter, chuckling. "When we were coming up the front steps, she insisted that the glow in the north was from the northern lights." Then, changing the subject, he said, "We drove Mrs. Hall and Nancy home from the show. She told Mother that Ted had been over to see you, and we both were expecting to see the front door standing open when we came home."

Andy poured out another handful of popcorn and said, "I closed it before the house got cold."

His father settled himself on a big wooden box with a padlocked lid in which Andy kept the parts he was accumulating for his amateur radio transmitter. It was not because he mistrusted any of the family or any other boy interested in amateur radio that he kept the parts box locked. It was just that some of those parts were fragile as a fine watch—like his voltmeter, for instance —and if *that* got dropped it was liable to crack a pivot jewel.

Finally his father said, "Did Ted have something special on his mind—some problem about the football team, perhaps?"

"If he did," said Andy evasively, "I'll get it, a piece at a time, between now and the Crawford game next Friday. That is, if I can keep track of the pieces." He wasn't anxious to have his father hear about the feud.

His father said hastily, "I'm mixed up in this matter, too, Son, which is the reason I asked. Thought we'd better go into a huddle over it so as not to get our signals crossed. Mr. Blair brought up the problem today when I was discussing a rather large insurance policy for his lumberyard."

With a note of alarm in his tone Andy said, "If all the fathers of the boys on the team take sides in this, it will be a mess."

"I agree with you." His father nodded. "Unfortunately Ken's father doesn't. Today I got in less than two minutes talking insurance with him and had to listen for a half hour about how the seniors on the team are so jealous of his son, who is only a junior, they deliberately try to make him look ridiculous every time he carries the ball."

"There has been some of that going on," admitted Andy uncomfortably, "but not for the reason Ken's father thinks."

Andy's father said, "I gathered from some rather— well—emphatic comments from Ken's father that Ted's attitude toward Ken isn't exactly cordial either."

Andy said, "Ken could be just about the top player in our conference if he would remember it doesn't matter too much who is carrying the ball if all eleven men on the team do their part."

"I gained the impression from Mr. Blair," said Andy's father, still guardedly, "that he heard much the same opinion from Ted when he talked the matter over with him recently."

Andy's father made an apologetic gesture with his left hand. "You and I are in an uncomfortable position, I'm afraid. Mr. Blair declines to accept Ted's view of the matter. He wants to talk to you about it."

Andy's only personal contact with Ken's father had been up in the stands, two weeks back, at the Grant game. The idea of having to face that dominating and forceful personality alone was alarming, to say the least.

"I think I know how you feel about it," said his father, dropping a hand on Andy's knee. "For business reasons I couldn't come out with a flat refusal——"

"What's business got to do with high school football?" demanded Andy, more emphatically than he realized. "Look, Dad, you yourself just said at the table to-night——"

A disturbed look came into his father's eyes. "I'm sorry, Son, but your mother was right about the reason Mr. Skiles wasn't asked to come back this year as your coach. A few businessmen carry their business methods into their family life. I don't think you'll understand why, but a few fathers think their boys should be 'successful' like their fathers—even if it is only getting their names in the paper as the star of a high school football team."

Andy slammed the empty popcorn box into his wastebasket and said, "If I've got to talk 'business' with Ken's father, I'll give it to him straight. I'll tell him the whole team knows that he is the one who worked hardest to keep Mr. Skiles from coming back this year because he wasn't a 'success,' a winning coach. And I'll tell him that if he would shut up and stop talking to Ken about football this whole squabble would be forgotten by everybody in a week."

"I was afraid of this," said Mr. Carter, getting up

with a sigh. He tapped Andy on the shoulder with the back of his fingers. "I was wrong in bringing up the subject in the first place. If Ken's father tries to mix football with business again tomorrow when I take over a sample policy—— Well, never mind. Just forget the whole thing. Good night, Son."

Chapter 14

Riverford 3 (yes, 3), Kenyon High o. That was the final score of the game, which made one college football coach reach for the telephone and call, long-distance, an alumnus in Riverford to ask about this boy Beck out there who kicked twenty-five-yard field goals in a high school game.

That three-point score was made just two minutes after the game began. Rain had already started, and when his team bogged down on Kenyon's fifteen-yard line, with only one more down to make six yards, Coach Dorman sent in Beck to kick that field goal from ten yards back of the scrimmage line. After that the rain fell in sheets and neither team got inside its opponent's thirty-yard line again.

The score of the game following, with Crawford High, was entirely different. Riverford won what the newspaper at Crawford called an "upset" by a 28 to 21 score. Beck kicked the point after each of his team's touchdowns.

After the Crawford game sports reporters began commenting on the fact that Coach Dorman was either very fortunate or very shrewd—and probably both—in having two star quarterbacks like Ken Blair and Stan Marshall. Coach Dorman received several compliments from the press for the way he had used Ken to throw accurate passes and then, when the Crawford secondary loosened up to stop his passing attack, sent in Marshall, who directed a smashing ground attack.

Naturally it did not show in the statistics of the game that all the scoring was done while Ken Blair was sitting on the substitute bench listening to Coach Dorman pointing out where he should start throwing his passes next.

But Andy, who hadn't played even one minute in a varsity game this far in the season, was beginning to hope that, at last, Coach Dorman had found a solution to the feud between Ken and the seniors.

Anyway, Coach Dorman seemed unusually pleased with the score, because he came up behind Andy after the game, when all the other substitutes had run out to congratulate the first string, and gave him a hard crack on the back and said, "You're doing fine, Son!"

Andy thought he had been mistaken for Eddins from the back and turned around so the coach could see his mistake. But the coach squinted one eye just a little and said, "Don't worry, I knew whose back I was talking to," and pushed his way on in among the other boys.

The players on the varsity didn't say a word, even among themselves, about how all the scoring had been done while Marshall was in at quarterback. Except Walker, and the only time he mentioned the subject was when he came up right after the game and almost bumped Andy off balance and said, "Maybe somebody will see daylight after this."

Andy grabbed Walker's hard-muscled arm and gave it a shake. "Keep your mouth shut about it."

Walker turned as though he hadn't heard and yelled to Ted Hall, the team's student manager, "Hey, Doc, bring me a stick of gum! My mouth is dry."

And now the varsity team was drilling for the next game, with Plainfield. The first- and second-string varsity teams were at scrimmage forty yards back of where Andy was still practicing kicking field goals. He had grown bored with kicking easy ones from the twelve-yard line and had backed up to the twenty-five-yard line, and off to a slight angle, just to make it a little more interesting.

He had just kicked two field goals from this position when an unfamiliar voice behind him said, "What's your name, Son?"

Andy turned around to find the sports reporter of the local morning paper waiting for an answer. Standing beside the reporter was the paper's photographer.

"Andy Carter," said Andy. He nodded upfield. "The regulars are all up there with Coach Dorman."

"We've already been up there," said the reporter. "Right now I'm interested in a fellow who has a pretty accurate toe." He nodded toward the practice goal posts. "Let me see you split 'em the way you were just doing."

Andy said, "Don't expect too much. I've never tried many from this far back."

"That's all right. I've seen professionals miss easier ones," said the reporter. "Just go ahead and try another one."

Andy turned, nodded to his ball holder and, when the ball was placed down, took one step and kicked. The ball cleared the crossbar by more than ten feet.

"Did you get it, Joe?" Andy heard the reporter ask his photographer.

"Think so, Mac," came back the answer.

As Andy turned around, the reporter's hand came out

of his jacket pocket in a sort of underhanded lateral passing motion.

"Souvenir for you, Son. Catch!"

Andy was still looking at a package of chewing gum as the reporter and his friend walked away toward their car. He poked the packet of chewing gum through a hole in his practice jersey and let it slide down to his belt.

Later, when he was changing clothes in the locker room, the package dropped to the floor. He picked it up and tossed it up on the metal shelf of his locker with the intention of giving it to Walker between halves at the Plainfield game the coming Friday.

The package of gum had scarcely landed on his locker shelf when the door at the far end of the locker room opened. Coach Dorman, holding a typewritten list, said gravely, "Let me have your attention, please!"

The chatter and laughter stopped as suddenly as though someone had snapped the switch of a radio receiver.

"All of you know that tomorrow is the first report-card day of the season," the coach went on. Then he paused to look around the room. "This is going to cause embarrassment to a few of you. But I think you would rather have your teammates hear the bad news before the rest of the student body hears it."

He glanced down at the list, shook his head regretfully, and started reading from it: " 'The following players on the varsity squad have failed to make passing grades in two or more full-credit subjects: Arnold, Beck, Jackson——' " The grave tone in Coach Dorman's voice grew even more noticeable as he spoke the last name, " '—and Marshall.' "

Marshall, the second-string quarterback, for whom the first team had scored all its points in the Crawford game, was standing beside Andy when his name was called. He turned slowly and began fumbling for his street clothes hanging in his locker.

"I sincerely hope this is only a temporary suspension from the squad," went on Coach Dorman. "Mr. McCall has arranged to give you deficiency examinations in your below-passing subjects next Friday. If you pass them satisfactorily, you will be permitted to return to the squad for practice the following Monday. Good luck to you."

The door had hardly closed behind Coach Dorman before Beck tossed his special-built kicking shoes to Andy. "These are yours now. I've been planning to quit school and get a job for a while. I sure need the money, and—well, take 'em, and good luck." He slapped Andy's shoulder.

Walker, a better-than-average student for all his muscular bulk, flung his own shoes into his locker and said disgustedly, "There goes our chance for the championship. I'll bet anything no player flunked off the Mansfield squad even if he made straight D right down his card!"

None of the rest, including Andy, had anything to say.

All the others had dressed and were gone as Andy started to close his locker—all but Ted Hall, who was hanging up the practice suit which Marshall had left lying on a dressing bench.

Andy stooped down and picked up the pair of kicking shoes that Beck had tossed to him. He started to put them in his locker with his own football shoes when Ted said, "I'll take Beck's shoes. There'll be more fellows moving up from the reserve squad for tomorrow's practice and those might fit one of them."

Andy said, "I'm keeping them. They're lucky. Beck hasn't missed a try for point with them all season."

"O.K., if you're superstitious," said Ted. "Keep Beck's shoes and give me yours."

Andy hesitated for a moment, then took his own shoes out of the locker and handed them over. "But I'll want them back if Beck's don't fit me."

"O.K., but make up your mind by the end of practice tomorrow," said Ted, and put Andy's shoes in the property chest and snapped the padlock shut.

When Andy reached home, Susie jerked the door open and pointed to the living room. "Look—*television!* Not one, but *two!*"

As though drawn by a powerful electromagnet Andy crossed the room and stood in front of the two television sets that were receiving the same program.

"It's a wedding anniversary present for Mother," said Andy's father.

"But why two?" asked Andy, still too dazed by the surprise to think of anything else to say.

His father rubbed his lip and smiled, a shade sheepishly, Andy thought, then said, "There wasn't time for me to take you down to the dealer's and pick out the one you thought was the better job. So he let me take them both home. Which one do you think we ought to keep?"

"I'll tell you which one I'd choose in a minute," said Andy. He went upstairs and came right down with his father's electric razor.

Susie laughed and said, "Are you going to give some-body in the studio a shave by television?"

Andy, assuming a grave professional air, plugged his father's electric razor into a baseboard electrical outlet and then wrapped the lead-in wire of one set around the buzzing motor of the shaver and studied the result-ing effect. He repeated the test on the other set. "I'd pick the one on the left," he said to his father.

"Never mind trying to explain, I wouldn't get it, any-how," said Mr. Carter, patting the set on the left. "We'll keep this one. Get the other one out of the room before we call in Mother."

Mrs. Carter's first reaction to her anniversary present was an affectionate smile for her husband and, "Will, you *did* remember, after all!"

With her hand under Mr. Carter's arm she watched the program for a minute or so, then said, "Turn it around a little, Andy, so we can all watch it from the dining room while we're eating. Come, everybody, din-ner is on the table."

Halfway through a drumstick of roast chicken Andy suddenly stopped moving his jaws and stared at nothing out in space.

"What's the matter—another expert trance?" in-quired Susie instantly.

"I feel a bad attack of TVI coming on," said Andy.

"If the Health Department tacks up a red sign and I can't go to school, I'll die before *you* do," was Susie's pessimistic prediction. "And all the sophomore varsity boys will catch it from you, because they are younger and more suspicious—well, more likely to catch things."

Their mother said, "I didn't think you looked at all

well when you came home tonight, Andy. You're probably worn out from trying to do too many things—school, football, working on your radio thing in the basement, helping at the garage on Saturdays——"

"Look!" said Mr. Carter, pointing to the living room. "Something has happened to the television set."

"Why, the picture is all scrambled!" exclaimed Susie.

Andy watched what was going on, then said authoritatively, "That's what I meant by TVI—television interference. That's from Mr. Harker's ham-radio transmitter, Station W9SPB, down the street. He must be using all his power trying to work his friend down in South Africa."

"Well, I *like* that!" said his father. "Here we put a lot of money into a present for your mother and somebody spoils everything. Call up Mr. Harker and ask him to stop doing that, Andy."

"Dad, I just *can't*," said Andy miserably. "Mr. Harker spent hours and hours teaching me to read code. And he gave me a copy of the wiring diagram of his transmitter, the one I'm building in the basement."

Their mother looked distressed when she said, "Will, the Harkers are such a lovely young couple, and they are both working to pay for their home."

"It isn't just our set," said Mr. Carter, already on the defensive. "I'll bet that thoughtless young fellow is spoiling the evening program for a dozen of our other friends." He fixed an uncompromising eye on Andy. "I don't care how you do it, but you've got to tell Mr. Harker that he is making enemies faster than a politician can shake hands at a circus."

"I'd rather someone other than a member of *this*

155

family told him," said their mother in that extramild tone she used on rare occasions. She gave Susie a special look. "And I don't feel that any of us should tell the neighbors—or even mention at school—what is spoiling their television programs."

Suddenly the television picture became normal again. A few moments later the telephone in the hall rang.

Susie jumped, saying, "That's probably Rocky Jenkins finally getting around to asking me to the *Goblins* party. I've been *hinting* until I'm practically frog-voiced about this."

She was back in a short time and obviously deeply disappointed. "It's Mr. Harker calling Andy," she said, and dropped into her chair again.

Gingerly Andy picked up the telephone and said, "This is Andy Carter."

Mr. Harker said, "Have you any idea how close to my house a Mr. Blair lives?"

Andy counted up the blocks mentally, then said, "About two blocks north of you."

Mr. Harker changed his direction of inquiry. "By any chance, do you folks have a TV set?"

"Yes," said Andy hesitantly, then added hurriedly, with a confirming glance over his shoulder, "but it's working fine now."

That last "now" from Andy was a mistake, because Mr. Harker immediately asked, "Was there any TVI showing a couple of minutes ago?"

In a weak voice Andy said, "A little. But we could still tell what the program was *supposed* to be."

"I was afraid of that," said Mr. Harker glumly. "I'll have to stay off the air until I make some harmonic traps and shield the rig better. Come over after lunch Saturday and help me, can you?"

"Send flowers to my funeral if I don't show up!" Andy said eagerly. He banged the telephone down on its cradle and almost ran back to the dining room. He picked up his drumstick and began eating ravenously.

"What happened?" his mother asked.

"I'm going over on Saturday," said Andy between bites, "and help Mr. Harker kill the TVI bugs in his transmitter."

"Don't bring any of the gruesome things back in your clothes," said Susie with a shudder.

"I was just thinking," said Mr. Carter, eying Andy steadily, "if Mr. Harker's amateur transmitter causes all that trouble with our set, one in *this* house would probably explode the picture tube. And they cost a lot of money, I understand."

Andy ladled some of his mother's golden chicken gravy over a split hot biscuit on his plate and said irrelevantly, "I think I'm going to like Ken Blair's father after all." He glanced across the table at his father. "He's the one who pulled me off the fire by calling up Mr. Harker about his TVI trouble."

"But how would he know?" asked Susie defensively. "I haven't told a soul yet."

"Mr. Blair is a very successful businessman with wide interests," explained her father cautiously. "He happens to be the silent partner in the radio supply house where, doubtless, Mr. Harker buys parts for his radio transmitter."

All their mother said was, "I'm glad Andy is feeling so much better," and smiled quietly to herself.

Chapter 15

Susie was camped in the living room in front of the new television set with a breakfast tray balanced on her knees and the soles of her scuffed saddle shoes jammed together. The comic section of the morning paper was spread out on the rug between her and the flickering television screen.

At the moment Andy came down the stairs to his breakfast, a young lady in an elaborate costume was praising the merits of a certain breakfast food against which Andy had an enthusiastic prejudice.

"If you're not watching, why don't you turn it off?" inquired Andy.

"I'll be looking again as soon as that silly person gets through invading my privacy," replied Susie. Then, without looking up, she beckoned to Andy and pointed with her chin to the sports page, opposite the comic page on the floor. "Why didn't you comb your hair before you let them take your picture?"

Andy stooped over for a closer look. "Mmmm—I did hit that ball just about right!" he mused critically.

Under his picture was a short paragraph reading, "Another reason why Coach John Dorman of Riverford is not worrying these days about losing games by one point because of a missed place kick after touchdown. He not only has 'Automatic' Beck, who has not missed a placement kick so far this season, but he also has 'Handy' Andy Carter ready to step into Beck's shoes at a moment's notice. 'Handy' Carter (shown above) must have rifle sights mounted on the toe of his kicking shoe, because he kicks thirty-five-yard field goals from difficult angles as easily as a veteran Marine Corps sharpshooter knocks over those little ducks in a shooting gallery."

"I don't think there will be a big Blair Lumber Company ad in Friday morning's paper, the way there usually is," remarked Susie as Andy finished reading the paragraph.

Just then their mother came to the entrance of the living room and said, "Andy, do you want a breakfast tray in there by the television set?"

"No, thank you, Mother," said Andy. "I'd rather be closer to the toaster," and went into the dining room.

In algebra class that morning Mr. Ellerly started his explanation of a new equation with his usual enthusiasm. But after observing Andy out of the corner of his eye moving his right foot and watching the toe of his shoe as though he were mentally practicing place kicks, Mr. Ellerly came to an abrupt stop and waited a long moment before remarking, "Mr. Carter, if a wad of chewing gum has become attached to the sole of your right shoe, you may be excused to remove the annoyance."

Andy blushed furiously and mumbled, "Excuse me, sir."

Mr. Ellerly continued his interrupted explanation.

At the end of the period Andy handed his report card to Mr. Ellerly and waited for the teacher to write in his advanced algebra grade. To his amazement it was an A! Ordinarily he carried his report card around in his hip pocket the way the other boys did, so that by the end of the day it was always rather badly wrinkled. But this time he put it inside his chemistry book; because, now that he had that A in his most troublesome subject, it was beginning to look as if he might take home the first straight A report card of his high school career.

By the time Andy reached his machine shop class that afternoon he had three more A's, and an A+ in chemistry. And when his turn came to be given his grade in machine shop, he placed his report card on the slanting top of Mr. Stark's stand-up desk confidently.

"Mmmm—Andrew Carter," mused Mr. Stark as though reading the name for the first time. He picked up a stub pen, dipped it slowly in an ink bottle, and made a big practice B+ on the corner of a scratch-pad.

Andy let out a subdued groan of disappointment.

Mr. Stark made another practice B+ on the scratch-pad. Slowly he laid down his pen and looked at Andy over the upper edges of his half spectacles. "I believe in grading a boy according to how near he comes to doing the best he can do—how hard he applies himself to doing his level best." He paused and shook his head. "I admit that you are quicker to learn, and that you are ahead of the class in completed projects. But a good many times I have seen you looking out the window toward the gymnasium when the other boys on the football team were coming out for practice. And I have had to speak to you several times about leaving your workbench not properly cleaned up before you rushed out to the gymnasium."

Mr. Stark gave a little grunt and picked up his pen again. "It goes against the grain, but I suppose I'll have to do it." He turned his pen point edgewise and made a small, thin-lined A on Andy's report card, then turned his back and walked away.

At the close of the machine shop class that afternoon Andy took extra care in cleaning up his bench, even to brushing some filings out of the vice screw, before going to the gymnasium locker room.

He put on Beck's lucky kicking shoes and trotted out to the practice field. They felt heavier and not so flexible as the ones Ted Hall had made him surrender the day before. And the cleats on the right shoe seemed to be shorter than those on the left shoe—or at least that is how it felt when he tried a short sprint after getting to the practice field.

But with his first attempt at kicking a field goal from the twelve-yard line he understood why Beck's kicking shoes felt different. The slightly shorter cleats on the right sole did not scrape the grass when he kicked. And the square box toe seemed to send the ball over the crossbar with less effort than he was accustomed to exerting.

After he had been practicing for some time, Coach Dorman walked over and watched him make five successful field goals without missing.

"That's the way I hope you kick points in the Plainfield game Friday," said Coach Dorman, nodding. "Keep practicing every minute so that you can do it without *thinking* about doing it right."

Then, before walking back to the varsity squad, he motioned to some of the other varsity substitutes standing around. "You boys rush in waving your arms when the ball is snapped, as in a real game."

The substitutes followed instructions enthusiastically —even adding a little touch of their own by bumping into Andy the moment after his toe struck the ball.

This caused him to miss several times. But finally he found that by keeping his eyes intently on the ball he did not even see the other boys rushing in.

Friday afternoon. The Riverford team had dressed in their own gymnasium and then traveled by chartered bus to Plainfield, twenty miles away.

Andy took his place on the substitute bench a few places down from where Coach Dorman sat watching the two teams line up for the first scrimmage after the kickoff, which Plainfield had chosen to receive.

There were some new faces along the substitute bench. Brown, the fast sophomore, had been moved up from the reserves as a substitute for Arnold, who had become ineligible to play. Sitting right next to Coach Dorman was Shorty Jones, the replacement quarterback for Stan Marshall, who was also ineligible. And, of course, Andy —wearing Beck's lucky shoes—permanently, because Beck had dropped school.

It soon became apparent that the Plainfield team was not going to score by line smashes through Riverford's all-senior line. On third down—standing almost in his own end zone—the Plainfield quarterback flipped a pass over the line to his right end. Eddins tackled the receiver on the thirty-yard line. It was a first down for Plainfield.

On the very next play the Plainfield quarterback faded back deep and threw a high looping pass to one of his halfbacks, who had cut in behind Ken Blair, Riverford's safety man.

The packed Plainfield cheering section sent up a shout of delight, anticipating a quick touchdown.

But the ball had been thrown against a stiff breeze. And just as it looked as if it were going far over Ken Blair's head, it suddenly started falling.

With an explosive burst of speed Ken whirled and caught the ball over his shoulder. The Plainfield halfback tackled him on the fifty-yard line.

Without waiting for a signal from Coach Dorman, Andy jumped up and started his limbering-up exercises —just in case. And when Ken—instead of attempting to carry the ball himself—sent Eddins crashing into the line behind Walker's charge, Andy was surer than ever that he soon would be kicking the first field goal of his career.

But the big Plainfield guard playing inside of Walker burst through and tackled Eddins at the line of scrimmage for no gain. Ken then sent his right halfback off tackle. But the other Plainfield guard threw him for a two-yard loss. . . . Then, on third down with eleven yards to go, Ken started one of his dazzling end runs.

The Plainfield defensive right end flung blockers aside with his big hands and bumped Ken out of bounds on the fifty-yard line. Ken dropped back and punted out of bounds on Plainfield's fifteen-yard line. Andy sat down again.

The score at the end of the half: Plainfield o, Visitors (Riverford) o.

Coach Dorman stood with his hands on his hips looking down at his team resting on the turf at the opposite end of the field from where the Plainfield team was gathered around its coach.

Coach Dorman said quietly, "This Plainfield team has the best defense we've been up against all season. They tackle for keeps, and we don't seem to be able to open up holes in their line."

"*I'll* say we don't," grunted Walker. "That guard playing inside me charges like a tank."

Cornstalk drawled plaintively, "Where do they get all those ends I keep seeing? I knock one down and another comes out of a crawfish hole in the ground and tackles our ball carrier."

Coach Dorman relaxed the firm lines around his mouth and said, "They are probably saying the same things about us down there at the other end of the field." He motioned for the squad to get on their feet. "You'll get stiff lying there. Get up and move around. Keep the pressure on. Remember, we're on our way to the first undefeated and untied season in Riverford's history. And we're not going to break the string today!"

After that Coach Dorman took Ken Blair aside—out of earshot of the rest of the squad—to discuss changes in offensive strategy for the second half.

Through most of the third quarter the rugged defensive play of both teams prevented either from scoring. Ken Blair was limping slightly. Eddins was showing signs of bone-weariness. And even Walker was moving back to the scrimmage line after the huddle without his usual display of relish for hard physical contact.

But Plainfield was also showing similar signs of tiring.

With only two minutes left in the third quarter, Coach Dorman suddenly slapped his knees with his hands, as though he had just made a difficult decision, and stood up. Sharply he called the names of an entire substitute line, including Brown's name. Then he named the new backfield, including Shorty Jones as quarterback, Rocky Jenkins as fullback—and Andy as right halfback!

The coach gave Jones a final slap on his shoulder pad and said, "Use Carter and his running pass on the first play."

Jones looked up and said, "You mean, from anyplace —even back close to our own goal line?"

"Use it anyplace Carter thinks he can pull it off without being tackled in the end zone," said Coach Dorman.

Just then Plainfield punted to Riverford's ten-yard line. Ken Blair hovered over the bouncing ball, waiting for it to roll on into the end zone so that it would be brought out to the twenty-yard line.

The ball rolled dead on Riverford's five!

"In you go!" said Coach Dorman, cracking his palms together.

The Riverford substitutes went into a huddle in their own end zone. Jones looked questioningly at Andy and said, "Now?"

Andy, remembering the position of the ball on the five-yard line, shook his head. "Give Jenkins a try first around right end. Brown and I will team up on their left end and drive him out."

"O.K., Rocky," said Jones, "make a little elbowroom for Andy on the next play."

With the snap of the ball Andy was off, running as fast as his stiff kicking shoes would permit. He drove his shoulder pad under the hands of Plainfield's defensive end. Brown missed his part of the block and raced on downfield.

The big Plainfield end flung Andy aside with a powerful sweep of his hands. But too late—Jenkins was already pounding downfield with the ball gripped in both hands. He burst through the tiring arms of a line backer. Brown bumped the defensive fullback aside, and Jenkins ran to the forty-yard line before he was dragged down by Plainfield's safety man.

In the next huddle Andy nodded to Jones. "This is the place. Remember, Brown—frog fingers!"

He got a perfect snapback from the center and raced parallel to the scrimmage line, making threatening passing motions as he ran. Brown was streaking down the side lines, but hadn't yet got far enough downfield to break inside behind Plainfield's safety man.

As the side lines loomed up in front of him, Andy saw that it was time to cut back and reverse his field for that long running pass. But when he tried to pivot on his right foot, the short cleats on Beck's old kicking shoes failed to hold. His feet flew out from under him and he fell with a stunning thud on the hard turf.

He rolled over, clawing frantically for the ball that had been jarred out of his arms. The Plainfield left end dived for it, but did not actually touch it before it rolled out of bounds.

"Riverford's ball!" said the referee. "Second down, and thirteen!"

Andy limped back to the huddle, a stabbing pain shooting up from his ankle with every step.

"Well, we gave 'em a good scare, anyhow." Jones grinned at his larger teammates towering over him.

On the next play he sent Andy out as the man-in-motion decoy, but keeping the ball himself on a quarterback sneak. He slipped past the big Plainfield guard who had been giving Walker so much trouble and was literally picked up in the arms of the intensely disgusted Plainfield fullback—but only after scampering thirteen yards for another first down.

Andy's ankle was paining him more after that last block which he had thrown on a Plainfield line backer.

Jones looked questioningly at him in the huddle. "Ready to try the running pass again?"

Andy shook his head and looked down at his right ankle, his pivot foot. "Wait a couple of plays until I get over this," he said.

On straight line smashes Riverford's substitutes almost made another first down.

But not quite; Andy dropped back on fourth down, gritting his teeth to brace himself against another searing stab of pain when his right foot struck the ball and got the kick away.

Plainfield's two guards and an end came charging in and knocked him back on his shoulder blades.

"Fifteen yards for roughing the kicker," announced the referee, and paced off the penalty. "Riverford's ball, first down!"

Andy was wondering how he was going to stand the pain of walking to the next huddle when Eddins suddenly slapped him on the shoulder and pointed to the side lines.

Then Walker, racing past him as he tightened his chin strap, flung over his shoulder, "Get a move on you. The Marines have landed!"

Andy did not see Ken Blair pivot close to the side lines, whirl and race back to the middle of the field again to throw one of his long, accurate passes into Cornstalk's waiting hands. That was because he was leaning over watching Ted Hall remove his kicking shoe.

But he did hear an excited cheer from the small group of Riverford rooters that had come to the game. He looked up just in time to see Ken Blair kneeling to receive the snapback from center for the try for point after touchdown.

Eddins' kick failed.

Coach Dorman got up and walked down to where Ted was wrapping an elastic bandage around Andy's ankle.

Andy looked up and said, "I'm sorry, Coach, about slipping——"

Coach Dorman gave Andy's shoulder a friendly tap with his hand and said, "You substitutes did all right. You gave the first team a six-minute rest. If they can't win this game from those dog-tired Plainfield boys, I'll *start* you substitutes next Friday."

That evening when Andy came limping gingerly up the front steps, Susie opened the door before he could touch it.

"Riverford 6, Plainfield o!" she shrieked. "What a game! And, in case you didn't know it, Rocky Jenkins finally asked me to the *Goblins* party. I've got to go right up and start dressing."

Andy grinned when she paused to say, "I'm sorry about your ankle, by the way," and then pranced up the stairs.

Chapter 16

Wednesday afternoon following the Plainfield game
Andy was practicing kicking field goals again. His ankle
was still taped, but with Beck's heavy shoes tightly laced
it gave him no discomfort.

He had been practicing but a few minutes when
Coach Dorman walked over to him and said, "How is
that ankle?"

"It's going to be all right by Friday," said Andy.

"You haven't been running to school on it?" asked the
coach.

"No, sir. It doesn't hurt so long as I walk sort of flat-
footed," said Andy.

Coach Dorman looked down at Andy's right foot and
said, "Better not do any more kicking today. Do about
ten minutes of grass drill, then come over and act as
head linesman for the scrimmage. I'll blow my whistle
when I want you."

What the coach called "grass drill" was lying on your
back, propping up your hips with your hands, and
pumping your feet into the air with a bicycle-riding motion; then putting your hands back of your head while
lying flat on your back and coming to a sitting position
without raising your heels from the ground. Next you
rolled over on your stomach, held your body rigid, and
pushed up with your hands. You did these exercises ten
times, stood up for a one-minute rest, then repeated the
series of exercises until the coach told you to stop.

Andy was on his third round of grass drill when Coach

Dorman blew his whistle as a signal for the varsity squad to take their places for the last scrimmage before the Walton game.

"Call every offside and any other illegal playing that you see," said Coach Dorman. "Watch for illegal use of the hands on offense particularly. Some of the other games in the league have been getting rough, and the officials are going to crack down harder from now on."

On the very first play Andy whistled shrilly through his teeth and pointed at Walker. "Offensive holding in the line."

Walker flung an indignant look at Andy. "Go soak your head. I've been doing that in every game since the Mansfield game last year. No *real* official has called me for it yet."

"What were you doing, Walker?" asked Coach Dorman.

"Just this," said Walker, dropping down on one knee to demonstrate. "When I'm blocking to hold the defensive guard on my side from drifting with the play I jam his toe with the palm of my hand, as if I were saving myself from falling."

"It's illegal. Stop it," said Coach Dorman.

A few plays later Andy saw Walker repeat the illegal act. He hesitated a moment, then whistled and pointed. "Offensive holding in the line—Walker again."

Walker took an angry step toward Andy. "Say, listen ——"

"Shut up, Walker," snapped Coach Dorman. "I saw you myself that time."

Sullen, rebellious anger blazed in Walker's eyes.

"Listen, Coach, the whole Mansfield line pulled that trick all last season, and they're pulling it again this year. If we don't give 'em back their own medicine, they'll run all over us."

"We play according to the rules on this team," said Coach Dorman curtly. "One more foul like that and you'll watch the Walton game from the substitute bench, Walker."

Walker shrugged and went back to his line position. For the rest of the scrimmage he charged furiously but legally.

In that half hour as head linesman Andy had kept a close watch on every play. Among other things he noticed that Walker had fallen into his old habit of shifting one foot or the other just before charging. And he had noticed something else—Ken Blair had acquired the habit of clapping his hands three times whenever he was sending the team out of the huddle for a long forward-pass play.

This new habit of Ken's was scarcely noticeable because of the intense purpose to win that he displayed every moment he was playing football, whether in practice scrimmage or in a real game. But Andy just couldn't go up to Ken and tell him what he had seen—especially right now when it was beginning to look as if the seniors on the varsity were willing to call off their private feud with their junior quarterback.

But that foot-shifting habit of Walker's was an entirely different problem for Andy. All he had to do was wait until the big tackle came growling up to him in the locker room after practice, then give it to him straight from the shoulder. Walker was like that. He spoke what was on his mind, and if you didn't like it that was your business, not his. If you wanted a fight, that was all right with Walker. If you cared to let the matter drop right there, that suited Walker, too. Five minutes later, just as likely as not, he would be around to borrow a stick of gum from you as though nothing had happened.

Andy was still thinking over these two new problems in the locker room after practice when Walker came up and bumped him with his shoulder. "Hey, where's your private detective's license, Hawkshaw?"

Andy looked Walker in the eye and said, "How mad at me are you?"

"Plenty," said Walker, staring back without blinking, "but not mad enough to slug a guy with a crippled foot."

Andy grinned slowly and pointed down to Walker's feet. "You've been talking with those two big coal barges again. Maybe that's why that Plainfield guard stopped you cold for nearly three quarters of the game."

Walker frowned down at his feet, then held out his hand without looking up. "Got a stick of gum on you?"

Andy reached up on his locker shelf and handed him the package of gum that the sports reporter for the morning paper had given him the week before.

Walker peeled three sticks, handed the other two back to Andy, and munched thoughtfully—still looking at his feet.

"Yeah, that was why," he said, nodding a single jerky nod. Then he looked up at Andy. "Was I doing it again today?"

"You were," said Andy.

Just then Coach Dorman spoke up coldly from behind Andy. "What's the difficulty between you two old friends? I thought I heard someone offering to slug someone else."

Walker ignored the tone of rebuke in Coach Dorman's voice and pointed down at his own feet. "Andy was just telling me I've been telegraphing my charge to the defense by shifting my feet."

Coach Dorman glanced quickly at Andy, who nodded. The coach rubbed his chin with his hand and turned away.

By the time Andy finished taking his shower, Ken had already dressed and left for home. And by the time Andy reached home himself he had all but forgotten about Ken's newly acquired habit of clapping his hands.

The headlines of the morning paper on Saturday after the Walton game read, RIVERFORD ROLLS ON UNDEFEATED: CRUSHES WALTON 28–0!

Andy kicked four perfect one-point field goals in the Walton game wearing Beck's old lucky shoes.

The sports reporter from the morning paper did not mention it in his story, but Walton received four fifteen-yard penalties for illegal use of the hands—two of which came within their own twenty-five-yard line and helped materially in setting the stage for two of Riverford's four touchdowns.

As Walker said after the game, "It was like getting paid for going to Sunday school. Hey, has anybody got a stick of gum?"

The sports reporter, however, did have something to say about Walker: "Riverford's big senior tackle,

Walker, cheerfully tore big holes in the Walton line for any Riverford back who happened to be carrying the ball. Time after time he gave Ken Blair a wide-open opportunity to display his ability as a broken-field runner. And any time Riverford's star quarterback wanted all the protection a man can ask for he stepped over behind his 'Iron Curtain,' Walker, and took his time picking out a receiver."

There was also a picture of Ken Blair crossing Walton's goal line through a gaping hole opened up by Walker.

The moment Andy saw that picture in the morning paper he was almost sure that the feud between the seniors and Ken Blair was all over.

Now came the final week of practice before the crucial game of the season with Mansfield High, unbeaten and untied! Riverford merchants used the slogan MASH MANSFIELD! in their advertisements and on banners pasted to their show windows. The equally partisan merchants of Mansfield took up the battle cry RUIN RIVERFORD!

Originally the game had been scheduled at Riverford's football field, which had a seating capacity barely large enough to accommodate the combined student bodies of the two schools. But on Monday before the game the demand for tickets by the general public exceeded the seating capacity at Riverford.

So, after a long-distance conference with the principal of Mansfield High School, Mr. McCall released the announcement to the press and three radio stations that the game would be played in the Sycamore College stadium, located midway between the two embattled communities, where fifteen thousand spectators could be accommodated.

The Monday-morning Riverford paper put the issue squarely up to the Riverford football team and its coaches in an editorial on the front page: "With the exception of Beck, the leading placement-kicking specialist of the Central High School Conference, Riverford is at the peak of its strength for the season. Three valuable replacements on the squad have made up their scholastic deficiencies and are again in perfect playing condition. Ken Blair has at last recovered his last year's skill at passing and broken-field running, and the all-senior Riverford line enters the fray as seasoned veterans.

"Coach Dorman, while not predicting victory for his boys, is perhaps the least perturbed at this hour of any adult citizen of Riverford who takes the slightest interest in football. He admits that he has a capable substitute for every one of his first-string players. And just recently he discovered another kicking specialist in Mr. Winthrop's reserve squad capably filling Beck's old shoes in the last two games, 'Handy' Andy Carter, who not only has rifle sights on his kicking shoe but can do several other things with a football.

"So, without intending to detract any credit or glory due the Mansfield team for its perfect record thus far in the season, we hope that 'this is the year' for championship-hungry and deserving Riverford High."

Copies of this editorial were fastened with pieces of adhesive tape to all but one of the locker doors in the locker room when Andy dressed alone that Monday afternoon for football practice. He made the display complete by taking his clipping of the same editorial and fastening it to the door of his locker with some bits of adhesive tape which he found on the floor under one of the dressing benches.

Then he sprinted out to the practice field, where he immediately lay down on his back to start his warm-up "grass drill."

He was pumping his feet in a bicycle-riding motion above his head when he saw Coach Dorman's hand reach out and grasp his right kicking shoe.

Coach Dorman examined the worn-down cleats and tested the stiffness of the leather in Andy's shoe, then said, "No wonder you slipped trying to pivot on that running-pass play against Plainfield. How's that ankle, by the way?"

Andy banged the heel of his right shoe on the ground by way of proof and said, "Just as good as ever. Even stronger, I think. I've been doing extra setting-up exercises every night before going to bed."

Coach Dorman frowned at the foot he had released. "See Ted Hall before you leave the gym tonight and get a pair of *running* shoes. And don't let me see you in those old clodhoppers again!"

When Coach Dorman used that tone, you didn't dare talk back. Andy got to his feet and, after watching his coach walk back toward the varsity squad, began his daily place-kicking practice.

But something had suddenly gone wrong. He could get distance and height, but in his first five attempts he missed kicking the ball between the goal posts by inches. Sometimes it veered to the right; then, for no apparent reason, it would veer to the left.

"Like the rest of the squad, you're pressing—too tense," said a voice behind him.

He turned to see Mr. Ellerly standing with his hands on the belt of his trousers. He removed one hand and gestured upfield. "Forget about kicking for today. You'll only fix your new bad habit of slicing the ball by continuing. Go upfield and take part in scrimmage drill."

Coach Dorman already had the varsity squad gathered about him when Andy arrived in time to hear him say, "I'm not scolding you, because I've had the same experience myself before the big game of the year. But you've all got the jitters. You linemen are lunging but not moving your feet. You backs are fumbling the ball because your fingers are tense."

He flipped a football over his right shoulder and caught it behind his back with his left hand and went on, "I am not going to give you any magic trick plays to beat Mansfield Friday. You're going to do it with good blocking and tackling—with *teamwork,* using the same old plays that every team you've beaten so far this season *knew* beforehand would be used against them."

An odd smile flickered across Coach Dorman's face. "We're going to try something different today. The backfield men will change places with the linemen, and the linemen will work as backs. I want all of you to go into this game understanding how tough is the other fellow's assignment."

The last thing Coach Dorman said before the two varsity teams lined up in their "scrambled positions" was, "Be careful of injuries. No clipping, absolutely. And make no tackles or blocks after you hear my whistle."

Andy found himself lined up as a guard facing Ken

Blair. And on the very first play big Walker, now playing fullback for the first time in his life, started a bull-like charge into the line.

With an easy flip of his hands Andy bunted Ken aside and met Walker head on, knocking him back on his shoulder blades.

Deliberately casual about it, Andy picked up the fumbled ball and tenderly helped Walker to his feet with his other hand. "Naughty, naughty," he said, brushing dust off Walker's shoulders. "I'll have to give you a traffic ticket for driving on the wrong side of the road, young man."

Walker snatched away the ball and said, "Run for the hills, little boy. I'm going through that same hole next play."

As Andy lined up again, Ken looked across the scrimmage line at him and said, "How did you get by me that easily?"

"Watch me this time and maybe you'll get wise," said Andy, and grinned—he had played just about every position on the team at one time or another trying to win his letter.

True to his promise, Walker came smashing at the same spot again. Andy ducked under Ken's charge and raised his shoulders, spread-eagling his opponent on his back. Walker crashed into their compact bodies; and Shorty Jones, who was playing end on Andy's side, tackled him before he could regain his balance.

When they got up, Andy saw a thin trickle of blood on Ken's upper lip. He straightened up as though to call Coach Dorman's attention to the injury. But Ken jerked his arm and said tensely, "Keep your big nose out of this," and when the ball was again snapped, he charged furiously into Andy.

A couple of plays later Ken came racing back out of the line, clapping his hands and barking, "Wake up, everybody!"

Andy gave Ken a quick look as he crouched for his charge and said, "Thanks," then broke through and tackled Cornstalk, who had dropped back for a long pass five yards behind the line of scrimmage.

"I think that's about enough to give you the idea," said Coach Dorman, picking up the ball that had been knocked from Cornstalk's hand. "Everybody back to his proper position for signal drill. No hard contact this time."

Ken pulled at Andy's arm. "Say, tell me something. Why did you say 'Thanks' when I lined up for that pass play?"

This was the opening that Andy had been waiting for. He chose his words carefully. *"Because you gave away the play* by coming out of the huddle clapping your hands three times."

A blank look swept over Ken's face. "When did you ever spot me doing that before?" he demanded.

"You started it back in the Trenton game," said Andy, "and you've been doing it ever since."

"I don't believe it!" was Ken's instantaneous reaction. "I've always been careful not to even push up my throwing-arm sleeve or even look where I'm going to pass—— Wait a minute!" He stopped short and frowned thoughtfully at the ground, then flashed a quick, unsmiling look up at Andy. "That *could* be why those Plainfield backs knocked down every one of my long passes."

"Except the one good one you pitched for a touchdown," said Andy.

Ken started to turn away, then tossed back over his shoulder, "That was *your* pass. I was just throwing it because none of my own were hitting."

That night at the dinner table Mr. Carter looked across at Andy, who was trying to read his amateur radio magazine and eat his custard dessert at the same time, and remarked dryly, "At least there is one person in Riverford who isn't thinking about football right this minute." He turned to his wife, adding, "This is going to be the poorest week I've had for closing contracts. You just can't get anybody to talk about anything but how the game is coming out."

Andy pinched his thumb down on a wiring diagram for clearing up television interference in an amateur radio transmitter and said, "Quit worrying, everybody. We *can't* lose!"

Susie looked across the table at her mother and said, "What do they call those people who wear a turban and can tell what's going to happen Friday just by looking into an empty goldfish bowl?"

Andy picked up his custard and his radio magazine and retired to the living room, where a program was being received on the new television set, saying, "There's too much Q.R.M. in here for me," but not bothering to explain what "Q.R.M." meant—too many people talking at once.

Chapter 17

Riverford's football players dressed in their own locker room before boarding a chartered bus for the fifteen-mile trip to the Sycamore College stadium, where the final game of the season was to be played against unbeaten and untied Mansfield High.

Andy was wearing his original pair of flexible, long-cleated backfield shoes, but with misgivings. Twice he had asked Coach Dorman to permit him to wear Beck's lucky kicking shoes. The first time Coach Dorman had said "No!" abruptly and gone on fastening the strap around a battered old suitcase. The second time Andy made the request, his coach said more patiently, but still firmly, "I want you in *running* shoes today. I may have to call on you for that long cutback pass of yours."

Coach Dorman was the last passenger to board the bus; while Andy, who had preceded him, walked the full length of the aisle and squeezed into a back seat between two fellow substitutes.

The battered suitcase which Coach Dorman seemed to cherish with great care, because of the way he held it on his lap, became a welcome subject for speculation as the bus rolled along. Any other subject—but not football —would have done just as well, because every player on the bus—including Andy, who could not help looking down at his running shoes every few minutes with a worried frown—was trying to pretend that *he* was taking this crucial game in stride.

Cornstalk started singing a doleful cowboy ballad in a

twanging drawl, with Rocky Jenkins providing an imitation of the guitar accompaniment by humming through his nose.

About the third stanza of Cornstalk's performance Walker interrupted him by elbowing his way forward and giving Coach Dorman's shoulder a shake, then pointing to the battered suitcase. "Hey, Coach, got any chewing gum in that thing?"

Coach Dorman restored the suitcase to its original position before Walker's push against his shoulder and said noncommittally, "No chewing gum, Walker. See your student manager, Ted Hall. All I've got in here is my lucky blanket."

"Yeah, like Andy's and Beck's shoes," grunted Walker, his curiosity completely satisfied. He elbowed his way back down the aisle, growling, "Who's got gum?"

Jones, the diminutive third-string quarterback, held out a single stick and said, "Here!"

Walker brushed Jones's hand aside. "I mean a whole package," he said, and went back to his seat.

Andy poked Ted, dressed in his sheepskin windbreaker and with the soles of his street shoes resting on top of his manager's supply kit. "Give Walker a package of gum. Maybe he's getting the jitters."

"He's already had one stick, like everybody else," said Ted, very businesslike. "He'll have to wait until the game starts for another."

In a dressing room under the Sycamore College concrete stadium five minutes before sending the team out onto the field for limbering-up exercises Coach Dorman read the names of the starting line-up.

He read ten names, then paused and looked down at Andy's running shoes. ". . . and Carter at right half," he added, then turned to Blair. "Use Carter mostly as a blocker to soften up those two fast Mansfield ends and the secondary," he said. "I'll send in a break-way runner later."

"How about passes?" asked Ken.

"Pass any time the secondary pulls up too close," said Coach Dorman.

"Except when Parks is in there," Andy blurted out without thinking.

Coach Dorman snapped a look over at Andy. He stared intently for a moment, then nodded curtly. "I've never seen Parks in action, but if *you* say he's that dangerous, we'll be careful."

Ken nudged Andy and, in a whisper, asked, "What makes Parks so tough?"

"Fast and dangerous," said Andy, motioning vaguely with his hands. "He can do anything with a football except turn it inside out and fly it over the goal line like an airplane."

Ten minutes of the first twelve-minute quarter had gone by scoreless. Ken Blair, facing his team, who had their backs to the scrimmage line, looked over Mansfield's defense and said, "This is the spot for Eighty-three. But this time Eddins takes out the end, who'll be watching for Andy. Get me one good downfield block, Andy, and I'll shine your shoes for the rest of my life if we don't score! Let's go!"

"Let's go!" repeated Ken, and clapped his hands sharply as the team ran back to the scrimmage line.

Andy, running a stride ahead of Eddins, who had purposely slowed down to allow him to catch up, fixed his eyes on the Mansfield left end's thigh pad and launched his block—but at the last moment he pivoted hard on his right foot for a break downfield.

His heart skipped a beat as he felt the cleats of his right shoe slip a little before they got a firm grip in the turf. He stumbled momentarily, caught his stride again, and headed downfield for Mansfield's triple-threat safety man, Reynolds.

Reynolds saw Andy coming and coolly started drifting, watching the blocker bearing down on him out of the corner of his eye but keeping his attention centered on the ball carrier.

Andy knew it was about time for Ken to make one of his quick side-stepping changes of direction and took a chance—cutting in toward the middle zone of the field even while Reynolds was still drifting toward the side lines.

Suddenly he saw Reynolds' eyes widen with alarm. That was the moment Andy had been waiting for.

Reynolds felt soft and relaxed as Andy's shoulder drove him across the side lines and out of bounds. And before Andy got up again, Ken had crossed the goal line!

Fifteen thousand spectators were sending up a mixed roar of triumph and dismay. But neither Andy nor his teammates were conscious of it as they lined up on the two-yard line for the try-for-point kick after touchdown.

Ten yards back of the ball Andy glanced up just once

at the crossbar, then fixed his eyes on the spot where Ken was to set down the ball. . . . Suddenly there it was! He swung his foot into it.

The field judge flung up his arms—good! Score: Riverford 7, Mansfield o.

Another right halfback raced onto the field from the Riverford bench. Andy peeled off his helmet as he raced to the side lines.

He was heading for the farther end of the bench when Coach Dorman called through his cupped hands, "Up here, Carter!"

Andy's knees gave way under him as he slumped down on the bench.

Coach Dorman caught one of Andy's trembling hands. "Are you hurt—was it that ankle again?"

Andy stared at his trembling hands, then began to grin sheepishly. "No, just scared silly," he said. He thrust out his kicking foot, clad in his old running shoes. "I didn't remember until after the ball was in the air that I didn't have on Beck's lucky shoes!"

Coach Dorman peeled a stick of chewing gum and handed it to Andy without comment.

Marshall, sitting next to Andy on the bench, gave his hair a gleeful scuffing with the heel of his hand. "Man, it was beyootiful the way Ken fooled Reynolds into thinking it was going to be a running pass!"

Andy looked down at his hands. They had quit trembling.

Although Mansfield failed to tie the score in the first half, the big, aggressive team in green and gold uniforms opened the third quarter with a whirlwind drive—line smashes and short passes by Reynolds that remorselessly pushed Riverford back to its own ten-yard line.

At that point Walker, who had been playing a methodical but thoroughly competent game, suddenly came raging through the line and tackled Reynolds so fiercely that he fumbled the ball. Ken dove over three men to recover it.

Ken got up groggily, walked a few steps, and fell flat on his face.

Coach Dorman sent in Marshall to replace him.

The team doctor examined Ken closely, then looked at Coach Dorman, who was standing anxiously over him, and said, "Very likely nothing but a bad jar. But——"

Coach Dorman nodded and said, "I won't," and went back to his seat on the bench.

With Marshall in as quarterback the Riverford team seemed to be playing as effectively as under Ken's leadership. Walker continued to tear holes in the grudging Mansfield line, through which Eddins plunged for short four-yard gains.

But when the Riverford drive had reached mid-field, the Mansfield coach sent in fresh men.

With a third down and seven yards to go, Marshall was in a strategic position to pass.

It was then—and too late—that Andy saw the new safety man for Mansfield was Parks!

He jumped up and yelled at the top of his voice, "Marshall! Check signals! Take a five-yard penalty, but *don't* pass."

The ball was already in the air. Parks, with wings on his feet, it seemed, skimmed around Cornstalk and snatched the ball inches from his flapping hands. . . . Not a Riverford would-be tackler touched Parks on the way to the goal line. Then, almost arrogantly, he dropped back and kicked a perfect goal. Score: Mansfield 7, Riverford 7. The scoreboard clock showed there were only six minutes remaining.

Andy turned a forlorn look of apology to his coach and said, almost sobbing, "I should have told you about Parks."

"You did," said Coach Dorman grimly. "And once should have been enough. That was my blunder for not sending in a substitute in time to warn Marshall."

As though to atone for his mistake, Marshall took the Mansfield kickoff and evaded all the Mansfield tacklers except one. Parks cut him down on the forty-yard line.

Coach Dorman reached out and dragged Shorty to him, motioning impatiently for Andy to drop down on one knee in front of him. "Jones, you replace Marshall. Carter, take over for Eddins; he's out on his feet." He gave Jones's arm another shake. "Act in the huddle as if you were calling the plays, but take your orders from Carter. In with you!"

"What's first?" asked Jones, standing in the quarter-back spot in the huddle.

"The running-pass play—only I don't pass," said Andy. Then, without turning his head, he said out of the corner of his mouth to Walker, breathing hoarsely beside him, "This will go for yards if you do the impossible —clean out two men for me."

At the snap of the ball Andy started for the side lines. Instantly Parks yelled to his line backers from his safety position, "The flying-bird play—*look out!*"

When he had almost reached the side lines Andy stabbed his right cleats into the turf and made his pivot to the right. However, instead of cutting back to the middle for his pass he made a complete spin and shot through the hole that Walker had opened for him.

Walker roared right on into another line backer, shaking Andy loose into the open. From then on it was a race between Parks, who had sprinted to the opposite side of the field to intercept an expected pass, and Andy.

Parks won the race at the twenty-yard line. As he released his vicelike grip on Andy's knees he grunted, "You *almost* fooled me. But you're too slow on your feet for my league."

As Andy trotted back to the huddle, the referee held up two fingers—indicating two minutes were left.

Little Jones looked questioningly to him for instructions.

"Place-kick. You hold, Jonesie."

"Yeah," panted Walker, near the point of exhaustion. "And while you're down on one knee, Jonesie, *pray!*"

The Mansfield team had never seen a field goal kicked from the thirty-yard line—and on first down, at that—especially with a long passer of Andy's reputation back there in kicking position.

Parks, their dynamic safety man, cracked his palms together and yelled, "Watch for a pass! But watch for *anything* from this guy!"

Perhaps they should have known from the way Andy's eyes were fixed on a tiny clover leaf that it was going to be a placement kick.

But the linemen failed to break through, and the

Mansfield ends hesitated too long while waiting for a possible pass or a running play.

Andy's right toe struck the ball with a satisfying thump. He did not have to look up to know that it was high over the crossbar and cleanly between the goal posts.

Parks rushed at him, half blinded by tears of mixed humiliation and admiration. He hit Andy with his fist on the shoulder pad, saying, "You thief, you——"

The referee grabbed Parks's arm and spun him around toward the side lines. "Out you go! This is a *game,* not a prize fight."

Andy grabbed the referee's arm and said, "You don't understand, sir. We were joking."

Andy's recollection of what happened in those last few explosive moments of the game was worse than any nightmare that he had ever had. Immediately after getting the ball on his own twenty-yard line, after Andy's field goal, Parks darted through a hole which Walker should have defended and raced to the fifty-yard line before Andy tackled him.

Two plays later again Parks evaded Walker, with a blocker leading the way. Andy spent too much time fighting off the blocker, and Parks flashed by to shake off Shorty Jones's ineffectual tackle and crossed the goal line standing up!

Heartsick, Andy turned his eyes away from his own goal line to see a red handkerchief down on the turf beside where Walker was standing.

Parks had already raced back to where the officials were gathered around the red handkerchief when Andy, as acting captain of his team, came up. It wasn't going to help much, he thought dispiritedly, because the penalty would be against Walker; Mansfield would refuse it and take the touchdown—and the game.

The referee took Andy's arm and shook him gently. "Defensive holding penalty against Mansfield's left tackle. What's your choice, Riverford?"

The offending tackle flung Andy aside and thrust his face close to the referee's nose. "How come you call defensive holding on me when we win the game? I been doing that all season and nobody's ever said 'boo' before!"

The head linesman turned to the referee. "This is the third time I've noticed this boy trying that trick. There was just enough question before to give him the benefit of the doubt. But this time it was too flagrant to overlook."

"I happened to see it myself," said the referee, and paced off a fifteen-yard penalty against Mansfield.

Two plays later the timer's pistol barked. Score: Riverford 10, Mansfield 7.

Walker turned toward the side lines. He took one step and fell flat on his face, completely exhausted.

Andy pulled Walker's limp arm over his shoulder and helped him to his feet.

Walker was sobbing. "He has been doing that all during the game—all during the game! I couldn't squeal on him, and I thought the officials would *never* see it. But they did, they *did!*"

With a wrench Walker broke loose from Andy's grasp and raked his sleeve across his eyes. "If you ever breathe a word of this baby act, I'll break every bone in your body!"

The Riverford substitutes swept Andy and the weary team into the stadium tunnel and on to the dressing room.

As the last member of the squad entered the dressing room, Coach Dorman motioned for Mr. Ellerly to close the door.

But before Mr. Ellerly could close it, the coach of the Mansfield team stepped inside. He lifted his hand. "I just want to say to a great aggregation of football players that you won that game cleanly and in a sportsmanlike manner. And the whole Mansfield team, including the man who drew that last penalty which cost us the Central High School Conference championship, all congratulate you. Mansfield is proud that it took as good a team as Riverford to beat us!"

Even before Coach Dorman could speak a word in acknowledgment, the Mansfield coach had left, closing the door behind him.

Coach Dorman stooped over and took his time about opening that battered suitcase which he had carried to the game.

He took out a blue blanket with a large gold block R in the center and held it up for all to see.

"When I first took over as your coach at the beginning of this season," he said, "I warned you that only eighteen major football letters would be awarded this year. I am compelled to keep my word——" He paused and looked the squad over, his eyes twinkling. "But I don't recall saying that there would *not* be a special, *and still higher,* award for the most valuable player on the team."

Again Coach Dorman paused and turned to Mr.

Ellerly. "Mr. Ellerly, what would you say were the standards by which the most valuable player should be selected?"

The suspense was too much for Ken Blair. He jumped up on a bench and raised both fists over his head. "Let's tell 'em, team, who it is!"

"ANDY!" roared back the team in unison.

There was a momentary hush as Coach Dorman smilingly started to toss the monogrammed blanket to Andy.

It was Walker's booming voice which broke the silence. "Hey, has anybody got any gum? Just *one* stick will do."

Suddenly Andy was upended by his teammates. They stripped off his running shoes; then put him down, right side up, on his feet again.

Cornstalk handed Andy's shoes to Coach Dorman and drawled, "Nobody will ever fill these shoes again like Andy. Hang 'em up in the Trophy Room of the gym."